I heard the pe... Citroën behind... to catch up. This was a good place for them to finish with me. Nobody around to see or hear.

But the old military road was perfect for my purpose, too. I gunned the Peugeot's engine and squealed around the tight turns, always climbing, staying far enough ahead as I neared the place I wanted.

Around a long hairpin bend I stopped the Peugeot and jumped out. The Citroën's driver wouldn't see my car blocking the way until he came around the bend. He would have to brake to a very sharp halt, directly in front of where I stood. I would be aiming my gun straight through the car window.

That was the way it *should* have worked. . . .

Fawcett Gold Medal Books
by Marvin Albert:

BACK IN THE REAL WORLD

THE STONE ANGEL

BACK IN THE REAL WORLD

Marvin Albert

FAWCETT GOLD MEDAL • NEW YORK

To Christine Joubert and the rest
of the gang at the fashion house
of Chloé in Paris
and
To Jean-Marie Juy, chief of the
Agence Privée de Recherches
on the Côte d'Azur
Merci Bien
M.H.A.

1

THE APPROACH TO Purgatory, according to Dante, resembles the cliffs around La Turbie.

Crow's house was atop one of those cliffs, high above the stretch of Mediterranean shoreline now known as the Côte d'Azur.

It was eleven o'clock on the last Sunday night in July when I dropped in on him and found the horror somebody had left there.

Crow's name was Frank Crowley. I still called him Crow because that was what everybody in our squad had called him in Vietnam. Back in those days we hadn't expected to wind up as neighbors on the French Riviera. Sometimes we hadn't expected to live to see the next morning.

My house was down near the sea, close to Monaco. Crow's was way up there near the entrance to La Turbie— a village dating back to the Roman Legions that engineered the first road across Dante's cliffs. More recent roads traverse them now. The three *corniches* run roughly parallel to the coast. Several narrower roads thread their way up from the Lower Corniche—the one nearest the shore below—to the Moyen Corniche, and then higher to the Grande Corniche.

The cliffs still plunge dangerously below the sides of the roads, and there is not much street lighting. So I was driving slowly as I approached La Turbie at eleven that night.

I hadn't planned to see Crow that late. I'd spent the

evening with friends who lived a few miles east, off the Grande Corniche. I was going home when I passed Crow's place. But then I saw his lights on, showing through the trees that hid his house from the road. And I remembered what he'd said earlier that day, something about needing to get things off his chest.

Fifty yards further along the right-hand shoulder of the road there was just enough space between a couple of plane trees. I pulled in very carefully, stopping with my wheels four inches from a two-hundred-foot drop.

As I walked back I considered the possibility that this might not be a good time for my visit. There was reason to believe he just might have female company other than his wife—though that didn't fit his normal pattern. I walked into his driveway first to see what was in his carport.

There was only one car. A four-door Opel Kadett. I didn't know it. I did know it didn't belong to either Crow's wife or the woman I'd thought might be with him. More peculiar was the absence of Crow's Citroën. Easiest explanation: he'd had trouble with his car, and the Opel Kadett belonged to someone who'd driven him home and was sharing a good-night drink with him inside.

I stood there and called out, "Crow?"

There was no answer. Only the noise of frogs and locusts.

He *could* be out by the pool behind the house and might not have heard me. I walked around the blind side of his house to the pool. Nobody there.

The pool patio ended at the edge of the cliff, with a view of the lights of Monaco fifteen hundred feet below. From that height you could see all eight square miles of it: from the palace hill across the harbor to its Monte Carlo section. A postage-stamp country, embraced by the last ridges of the Alps running into the sea on either side of it.

I turned my back on the view and looked at the lights of Crow's living room. They shone out onto the pool area through the sliding glass doors. One of the doors was wide open.

I tried again: "Crow?"

Nothing.

I moved to the end of the pool area and opened the little shed that held gardening tools. I took out a pair of clippers with sharp blades locked together and a short-handled shovel. The shovel I balanced in my right hand like a club while holding the clippers in my left like a dagger. I approached the open door to the living room that way. Feeling a little silly, but not much. There's a prickly sensation you get when you've been in the presence of death often enough. Sometimes it's wrong, but that's better than being dead.

There was nobody in the living room and nothing disturbed. I stood there for a time and listened. And heard nothing.

Light was on inside the main bedroom, too. I walked to its open doorway. Stopped there and looked.

They were both naked, their clothes scattered on the floor.

The man was sprawled on his back across the rumpled bed. The blood around the bullet wound below his breastbone still had a wet shine. There was another hole in his forehead from which a little blood had trickled into one of his wide-open eyes.

The woman was huddled on her side on the carpet near the door. She had tried to run away. She'd been shot between the shoulder blades and behind the ear.

A professional job. Just two shots for each. One in the body to knock the victim down, another in the head to insure death.

Two people who had stopped being people a very short time before I'd entered the house.

I knew them both.

I turned and went through the rest of the house, holding my makeshift weapons ready. They no longer felt silly in my hands. Just inadequate. I would have preferred an automatic rifle.

No one else was in the house. I found the front door unlocked. There was nobody lurking outside on the dark grounds. The Opel Kadett was still in the carport. I went back into the house and checked the room the Crowleys used as a study. The pistol Crow usually kept there in the back of the desk drawer was missing.

I returned to the main bedroom and looked again at the man and woman who had been killed there. Sorting out what I could tell the police when they arrived and which things I didn't want to tell them.

It had been a long Sunday. Containing encounters that took on more significance now than I had given them at the time.

I tried to work out what connection each of them might have to the way the day had ended, there in the bedroom of the Crowley home.

Starting with my running into Crow's mother-in-law, Mona Vaillant, that morning in Monte Carlo.

2

I HAD KNOWN Mona Vaillant for much of my life. Since long before her name became a prestige label in trendy women's wear shops from Paris to Dallas. I'd known her son and daughter just as long, and I was the one who'd introduced them to the people they married. Five people, each of whom I considered a close friend.

But nothing I knew about them, and nothing Mona told me that Sunday morning, held any forewarning that one of those friends would be dead before the next day and another charged with murder.

It hadn't been the best of mornings for me before my chance encounter with Mona. Ten minutes earlier I had finished a short-lived investigation for one of the reigning queens of Riviera society. More accurately, my client had terminated my employment, with extreme dissatisfaction.

Monte Carlo was gearing up for the most crucial part of its summer social season: the week that peaks with its Red Cross Gala, one event at which attendance by Prince Rainier and family is guaranteed. It is prime time for upper crust bitchiness and back stabbing. Jet-setters from places like Saint Moritz, Kuwait and Palm Beach converge on the tiny seaside principality that week to reconfirm their status. The game is to get themselves invited to the right parties and dodge those at which, rumors hint, the most coveted guests will fail to show. Excessively rich hostesses jockey

for position, their smiles and jewels glittering as they
sharpen hidden knives for the infighting.

My client was one of those hostesses. She suspected a
sneaky rival of trying to disrupt her plans by bribing her
staff. It has been known to happen, so I checked it out.
Three days convinced me she was wrong, in this case. My
report convinced her I'd been bought by her rival. She
decided to hire a more trustworthy detective.

I thanked her politely for taking her paranoia off my
back. She was in the middle of an unladylike remark when
I walked away from her and out of the building.

Our parting took place in the Casino of Monte Carlo,
where she was renting the downstairs Ganne Room to hold
a cocktail party for the cream of her guest list the following
weekend. My step felt lighter as I went down the entrance
steps into the Place du Casino. I walked around its circle
of flower beds and banyan trees to start my morning afresh
over a good cappuccino in the Hotel de Paris.

Like the Casino, the hotel was built in the plush years
of the late 1800s. The Art Nouveau opulence of the two
buildings now forms an oasis of old-world elegance in a
growing forest of high-rise office and apartment condos.
Entering the hotel's lobby I always feel I've stepped
through a time machine into a past era with a more gra-
cious, relaxed life-style.

I picked up a copy of that morning's *Nice-Matin* at the
porter's desk and went into the bar.

It's a soothing room done in muted colors. Dark brown
wood and light brown marble and leather; dark green
flower-patterned carpet, light green and beige draperies.
Tall windows framing views of palm trees against sea and
sky. That early on a Sunday I had a free choice of tables.
Only three were taken. Mona Vaillant was at one of them.

Seeing whom she was with gave me a jolt.

They were at a corner table off to the left of the entrance. The man was a rangy, sharp-faced blond in his mid-thirties. He had what looked like a Bloody Mary in his big hand. Mona was taking sips of tea while she listened with a troubled frown to whatever he was telling her.

She was half-turned from me and I saw her face in profile. It remained the classic profile so often photographed. She no longer allowed cameras to get close enough to register the delicate network of wrinkles. And she never permitted gray to show in her tawny hair. It wasn't vanity, it was part of her selling image. A lot of women bought Mona's clothes because they wanted to look like her. She always wore her own creations. That morning it was a pleated silk tunic and slacks, both in a cool floral print that gave a softened line to her lean figure.

She hadn't seen me come in. The man she was listening to had. The only indication was a narrowing of his eyes. Then he resumed talking to her. Not light conversation. It had to be business—his kind of business.

I ordered my cappuccino and took a table near the bar, settling into a leather-padded chair facing the windows at the rear of the room. That way I wouldn't be watching Mona and August Pilon.

He had been a *stup* until he'd quit the police to start his own one-man detective agency in Nice. A *stup* is what the French call a narc, *stupéfiants* being narcotics. With that kind of experience Pilon was street-smart and tough enough to handle whatever came his way. I had nothing against him. I just didn't like seeing him with Mona.

Having a neurotic celebrity-snatcher decide to fire me and hire somebody else that morning had been a relief. But having Mona Vaillant prefer the competition to me—that stung.

I'd been thirteen when I first saw her. That was the summer she came to our house below the coast road to ask for work as a part-time housekeeper. One thing my mother, Babette, loathed was any kind of household chores. So Mona Vaillant got the job—for the rest of that summer and the two summers that followed. Summers were the only time Babette and I spent at the house she'd inherited from her father. The rest of the year I went to school in Chicago, where I lived with my father's parents, and Babette was at universities in Paris, first as a student and then as a professor of art history.

Next to Babette, who was statuesque, Mona looked small and fragile. But she turned out to have a force of character equal to Babette's, which was considerable. They shared something else. Each had lost her husband to a war.

My father had been a U.S. Air Force tailgunner in World War II. He'd met and married Babette after bailing out of a crippled bomber and being picked up by her Resistance group. The war was in its last weeks when he died, four months before I was born.

Mona's husband had been killed the year before she came to us, in France's Algerian War.

He had been a career officer. There was a pension for his widow and two children, but it wasn't enough for Mona to keep their house in Nice and raise her kids properly. Doing housework for people like my mother was one of the ways she supplemented that income.

She always showed up with her son and daughter in tow. Gilles was a year older than me, and Nathalie four years younger. Usually I took them down to the cove below our house and we'd spend the day swimming, searching the beach for mussels, fishing off the rocks at the base of the sea cliffs. Sometimes we packed picnic lunches and went on all-day hikes into the mountains behind the Grande Corniche. Our friendship continued after their mother stopped working for mine, and we renewed it as adults when I finally left the States to settle in France.

The reason Mona quit doing housework, for us or anyone else, was that her other means of supplementing her income had turned into a full-time business.

Before her marriage she'd been a student at the Chambre Syndicale school of couture in Paris, expecting to become an apprentice designer-cutter when she finished the three-year course. Her career plans had been dropped to accompany her army officer husband to Indochina, where she gave birth to her children. But she always continued to make her own clothes. And after her husband's death she began making dresses for women she knew. The first Mona Vaillant creation I ever saw was an outfit Babette bought from her.

It was after she began selling her work through small shops in our area, from Menton to Cannes, that she dropped everything else for her resumed career. By the time I started going to the University of Chicago she had a real workshop in Nice, employing eleven assistants, and was selling her ready-to-wear outfits to department stores in Paris, Milan, and New York. By the time I finished my military service in Vietnam she was opening her own boutiques at choice locations in major cities.

Her choicest, and latest, was just around the corner from the hotel where I was having my cappuccino that Sunday morning: on the Avenue des Beaux-Arts. "Avenue" is an odd thing to call a one-block, one-way street barely wide enough for two cars. But it is flanked by names that make it *the* showcase shopping street of Monte Carlo.

The new Mona Vaillant shop was on the same side as Cartier, Givenchy and Vuitton, across from Christian Dior, Bulgari and Saint Laurent.

It took willpower not to turn my head to look at her and August Pilon. My willpower has more ebb and flow than the Mediterranean. That morning it rose to the occasion. I was proud of it. I drank my cappuccino and concentrated on the front page of *Nice-Matin*.

It's the only daily paper serving the entire Riviera. Disturbing world news gets short shrift on inside pages, hidden among sports events and local social gatherings. It is devoted to soothing its readers. That was fine with me. A man who has been passed over for his competitors twice in one morning can use a little soothing.

As usual, the front page was almost entirely taken up by several large color pictures of people enjoying themselves. A French soccer star relaxing with his family at a beach barbecue in Cannes. A German orchestra conductor trying out his new racing yacht off Saint-Tropez. An Arab prince escorting a Swedish model through an exhibition by a British sculptor at Saint-Paul-de-Vence.

There was also an advertisement for a new luxury condominium under construction a block from the Casino. It promised prospective tenants "the Nostalgic Decor of the Madly Sophisticated Belle Epoque Era and the First Anti-Atomic Bomb Shelter in Monaco."

Mona was standing beside my table, her smile warm but tentative. "You're upset with me."

I glanced toward her table as I stood up to give her a dutiful peck on the cheek. August Pilon had gone. "Not upset, Mona. Try angry. Also puzzled."

She pulled my face back down to hers and kissed me lightly on the lips. "You're beautiful when you're angry."

"That's supposed to be the man's line."

"Sometimes you sound like the worst mixture possible," she told me as she sat down. "Stuffy Frenchman and uptight American."

I found myself grinning. "Blood will tell." I settled back into my own chair. "Can I order you something?"

"No. Gilles will be picking me up here any minute. We have an appointment to see a luggage manufacturer from California. He wants a licensing agreement to produce a line of handbags using my label."

Her son Gilles was now her business manager. Though the Mona Vaillant enterprise kept expanding, it remained at its core a family business. Gilles's wife, Anne-Marie, was Mona's assistant designer. Mona's daughter, Nathalie, was chief of merchandising. Only Nathalie's husband, Crow, wasn't part of it; and even he pitched in to help when needed.

"Who's the luggage maker?" I asked Mona. She gave me the name, and I was suitably impressed. "Congratulations. Sounds like the latest chapter in the uninterrupted rise of Mona Vaillant."

She frowned, the way she'd been frowning while listening to August Pilon. "There *have* been interruptions."

"Recently?"

She hesitated. "Yes."

"Something you had to hire Pilon for?"

This time she didn't hesitate. She changed the subject. "You've been away most of the summer."

I nodded. "Five weeks." Most of that time had been spent in Italy, posing as a buyer for an American drugstore chain in order to nail a pirate company turning out useless medicines on which they put faked brand labels of a top pharmaceutical firm. "But I've been back almost two weeks, Mona. Maybe you didn't know. Or maybe you just don't believe in giving your business to old friends."

"You're more than a friend. You're practically family."

"Oh. That explains it."

She smiled. But it was forced. "You're getting that look again, Pierre-Ange."

Pierre-Ange was what my mother had named me: not an

unusual name in France. But when I'd started living with my father's parents they'd altered it to Peter—for which I was grateful. Pete was a lot more comfortable for a kid growing up in Chicago. Also later in the service, and when I joined the police force under the sponsorship of my grandfather, who was a captain before retirement. Pete or Peter: neither led to the kind of cracks some Americans came up with when they figured out that Pierre-Ange could be literally translated as Stone Angel—something that wouldn't occur to anyone French.

"I have that look," I told Mona, "because if you've got trouble you should have come to me with it. August Pilon is good at his job. I'm better."

"But you are also a friend to every member of my family. A good friend. And it's one of them who is causing the problem. I suspected that it had to be. What Monsieur Pilon just told me confirms that suspicion."

"Which one?"

"I don't know yet. I think Monsieur Pilon does, but he doesn't want to tell me until he's absolutely certain."

"Whatever the problem is," I said, "I'd handle it in a way that would give all of you the least hurt. Pilon won't."

"You might also be inclined to protect the one who . . . has done something unpleasant."

"Meaning you didn't trust me to tell you whatever I found out."

"I trust you as much as I've always trusted everyone in my family," she said with an edgy bitterness. "And *that* turns out to have been a mistake."

"It's that bad?"

She nodded gravely. "Very bad."

3

BEFORE I COULD pry any more out of Mona she said, quickly and quietly, "There's Gilles. Please don't mention this to him or to anyone else."

Gilles Vaillant didn't have the good looks of his mother or sister. He was almost my height but burly, verging on fat, and he'd started going bald in his twenties. His eyes were shy and his mouth was stubborn. He treated most people with a reserved politeness. But his warmth with the few he cared for went deep. He grabbed my hand with a welcoming smile. "Pete, how long have you been back?"

He liked to practice his English on me. He'd taken postgraduate business management courses in California and New York after finishing the Hautes Études Commerciales in Paris.

"A couple weeks," I told him, and I asked after his wife and son.

"Alain is visiting this summer with Anne-Marie's parents up near La Brigue. The mountain air is good for his sinus condition." Gilles sat down and added, with apparent lack of interest, "Anne-Marie is spending the day in Antibes with some new friends she's acquired. I believe they're going sailing."

Mona said to him, "I was just about to tell Pierre-Ange what Crow has done."

I had introduced Frank Crowley to the Vaillant family as "Crow", and they'd been calling him that ever since. Be-

13

tween Vietnam and his first visit to the Riviera Crow had built a reputation around Los Angeles as a genius at computer programming. He'd planned to spend a week's vacation as my houseguest and then return to his job. But he fell in love with the area—and with Mona's daughter, Nathalie. He sold out his interests in California, bought the house near La Turbie, and started a computer company in Nice with a French partner the week before he and Nathalie got married.

"What *has* Crow done?" I asked.

"He's quit his company." Mona's tone was worried—a different sort of worry than when she'd spoken of whatever Pilon was doing for her. "He suddenly sold his share to his partner and decided to retire."

Gilles made a placating gesture in his mother's direction. "Crow simply got tired of the daily grind. He needs some time off, that's all. It's not so terrible."

"He's talking about taking the rest of his *life* off," Mona retorted.

Gilles looked at me. "You didn't know about it?"

I shook my head. "I haven't seen Crow in a couple months. How is Nathalie taking it?"

Mona answered. "She's stunned. What would you expect? Nathalie married an exciting man with an enormous amount of drive and ambition. And then he suddenly announces he doesn't want to work anymore."

"You're exaggerating it," Gilles told her quietly. "There's his photography."

"That's his hobby, not his profession." Mona turned back to me. "I'd appreciate it if you talked to him. You've known Crow longest."

"Mama," Gilles said, "don't interfere. Let them work it out for themselves."

"There has to be something wrong with Crow," she in-sisted. "Nathalie thinks so, too. A man who is happy doesn't want to change his life so abruptly and drastically."

"Don't interfere," Gilles repeated uncomfortably. "When a couple has problems, the best thing everybody else can do is to keep out of it."

It sounded to me as if he was talking about his own marriage.

He looked at his watch and stood up. "We have to go now or we'll be late."

Mona nodded and rose to her feet. "Please talk to Crow," she asked me quietly. Gilles turned away and started out of the bar. Mona kissed me good-bye and said more softly, "And *don't* be angry with me—about that other matter."

I left shortly after they did. Outside there wasn't a cloud in the sky. The noon heat was a dense weight that felt like a load of lead across my head and shoulders when I stepped into the sunlight. I took off my jacket and put on my sunglasses before walking toward the garage where I'd left my car.

I went around the Place du Casino thinking about what Crow had done. And about what somebody else had done that was bad enough to make Mona hire August Pilon. Two family problems, but unrelated: Mona wanted me to talk to Crow, and she didn't want me to poke my nose into the other matter.

As I reached the other side of the *place* I suddenly stopped thinking about both problems.

Because I spotted Arlette Alfani having herself a rich desert on the terrace of the Café de Paris. And Arlette, doing anything at all or nothing at all, was one young woman capable of diverting a miser's attention away from a bright new stack of gold coins.

4

ALFANI HAD BEEN her maiden name. Now she was a contessa, and her last name was Vallaresso. The change had come with her marriage a year before to a young Italian nobleman she'd met in Paris. But I hadn't seen Arlette in two years—since she'd gone off to Paris to finish law school.

She had been twenty-five then, making her twenty-seven now. She'd changed her hairstyle. Two years before it had been long and flowing. Now it was cropped short and boyish. On her that was pure perversity. Nothing could make Arlette look like a boy.

She was making fast work of a sugar crêpe topped with gobs of whipped cream. The lusty appetite wasn't new: Arlette didn't believe in watching her figure. She reasoned that as long as enough other people watched it she didn't have to worry. Quite right. And still true, judging by what she did to make faded jeans and a V-necked T-shirt with deeply scooped sides look sensational.

Most people took a long time before noticing anything else about Arlette. Like the attentive eyes. Or the fact that her IQ topped out somewhere around the genius level.

Arlette saw me and was on her feet with her arms tight around my neck an instant later. I took hold of her supple waist and gently detached her pelvis from mine.

"Arlette, you'll get us arrested."

16

"Not here, darling. Only in Italy. You can get arrested for kissing your own husband in public there."

That seemed to remind her: she kissed me on the mouth, transferring some whipped cream from her lips to mine. She regarded that with a little smile. Then she used a fingertip to remove the cream from my mouth and sucked it between her ripe lips.

"Speaking of Italy and husbands," I said, "how *is* your Italian husband?"

Arlette sat down, tugging me into the chair beside her. "About to become my *ex*-husband," she told me matter-of-factly. "At the moment he's down at his palazzo in Sicily, sulking about it."

Half the married couples I knew seemed to be suddenly coming apart. I don't know why that aspect of modern life should have continued to surprise me. My own marriage had bitten the dust back when I was still working as a federal narc in the States.

I said, "Short marriage."

Arlette made a rueful face. "Giovanni thought it was *so* amusing, marrying a pretty girl who was smart enough to get through law school. He boasted about it to all his friends when we went to Sicily to celebrate after I won my degree. But when he realized I actually intended to come back to France and *practice* law as a full-time profession he wouldn't hear of it."

Anybody who tried to forbid Arlette to do something she wanted was in for a shock.

"Turned out he expected me to settle down and become a normal, do-nothing, upper-class Italian wife. My being a lawyer was supposed to be like knowing how to knit or sew. Not to be taken seriously. We fought about it, and . . . Well, here I am. And *there* he is, sulking. I should have known better than to marry an Italian."

"You're mostly Italian yourself," I pointed out. Most Corsicans, though French citizens, are of Italian descent.

"Maybe, but I don't work at proving it. Giovanni does."

"Where are you going to practice law?"

"Here. I already am. I'm a junior partner in the Bonnet law firm in Nice."

I was impressed. Henri and Joelle Bonnet were a husband-and-wife team acknowledged to be among the best attorneys on the Riviera. They represented Mona Vaillant's company and the company of Crow and his partner, among others. I had done investigations for one of their civil cases and several of their criminal defense cases.

"How long have you been back?" I asked Arlette.

"A few months. I tried to phone you, but you were away."

"That's fast work—only back three months and already a partner of the Bonnets."

"Don't try to sound naive," Arlette said. "My father *bought* me the partnership, of course. With more cash than they could possibly refuse. But I don't think they regret it. So far I've helped prepare the dossiers for a number of their cases, and they've been quite pleased. Surprised, too, I think. They're talking about letting me handle one of their simpler defense cases on my own soon, in court."

She attacked her desert again with open relish. "I have to get back to a brunch party in the penthouse of that building over there." She pointed at a modern high-rise whose architecture reminded me of a prison. "I sneaked down here because I don't like what they're serving. In fact, I don't much like the people there, either. But the host is an important client of the Bonnets, and they're off on vacation right now. So I have to do the necessary."

"Are Henri and Joelle Bonnet handling your divorce?"

"Probably, when I get around to it." Arlette shrugged.

"There's no reason for me to hurry it. Not unless I find myself getting involved with some very interesting man."

She gave me another of her small smiles. "Speaking of which, sir, I could be available tomorrow evening. I'm staying at my father's place until I find a good apartment. You could pick me up there and we could go for a night swim. Like old times. If you still like me."

"I still like you," I assured her. "But your father might not like my reviving old times with his married daughter."

"You're not afraid of my father."

"No more than everybody else. Everybody with enough sense not to step on a cobra."

"He would never hurt *you*. Besides, he's retired."

"Retired cobras don't forget how to bite."

Before his retirement Marcel Alfani had run half the rackets in Marseilles and Paris. He was the reason I'd lost my last and best steady job, as a European investigator for the U.S. Senate Foreign Relations Committee. They'd accused me of concealing evidence that Alfani was brokering crooked deals between French and American firms. I hadn't explained that I'd done it to pay off an old debt; the committee members wouldn't have been interested in that.

During World War II most French gangsters sensibly cooperated with the Nazi occupation forces and Vichy government. But Corsicans are rebels against authority by nature and history. Alfani was one who secretly aided the Resistance. When Gestapo agents were hunting for my mother, Alfani hid her—along with me inside her womb— in the attic of his classiest brothel. And when the searchers got too close, he smuggled pregnant Babette out of the country.

His daughter, Arlette, finished the last of her desert and stood up. "Got to get back." She bent and kissed me again. "See you tomorrow evening. Between seven and eight."

She didn't doubt that I'd show up. Neither did I.

I watched her walk away. I wasn't the only one. Every male head along both sides of the street turned as she went by.

I drove out of the Monte Carlo section of Monaco, down through the Condamine quarter behind its little port, and past the open food market and the hill that held the palace of Monaco's ruling family. Seconds later I was out of Monaco and back in France. There is no visible frontier between the two, no passport or custom control on either side. Only some Monegasque cops, in handsome uniforms, who occasionally stop a car they don't know to look at the driver's papers.

They knew me and they knew my car. It was a Peugeot 205 with a dented hood and a gash in the right front fender, both acquired when I'd skidded off a mountain road during the last Monte Carlo rally. I had no intention of doing a cosmetic job on those exterior blemishes, though I had repaired the extensive interior damage. The Riviera abounds in car thieves, because Italy is close, and once they get a stolen vehicle across the border your chances of getting it back are nil. That's why a lot of permanent residents prefer installing new engines inside battered hulks to buying new cars.

I drove west with the Mediterranean below me and the Maritime Alps above. Although it was the height of the tourist season, the traffic wasn't heavy at that time of day. By noon most of the Parisians and other vacationers were already packing the beaches with a display of flesh ranging from milky white to lobster-red. Some even had the coveted chocolate brown. But not many. Few of them ever went into the sea. Most were content to just stare at it whenever they shifted position to insure that no inch of skin went unburned. By that night a lot of newcomers wouldn't be able to put on clothes without shrieks of agony. Some would be in the hospital. Mad dogs and tourists.

Minutes from Monaco I turned down the private driveway that descended to my house. I had planned to devote the early afternoon to replacing a faulty valve in the water storage tank in the attic. After which I'd planned to take my daily workout: a long swim from the cove below the house. But I had changed my mind.

I stayed only long enough to get out of my neat summer business suit and into a loose-fitting T-shirt and an aging pair of tennis shorts. Shoving my bare feet into rope-soled espadrilles, I drove back up the steep slope to the Lower Corniche and continued west toward Beaulieu.

Crow and Nathalie usually lunched there on Sundays. I agreed with Gilles about not interfering. But each of the people in this particular couple meant a great deal to me. I wanted to get my own feeling of what the climate was between them.

⊠ 5 ⊠

THE HEART OF Beaulieu is the most flourishing marina anywhere along the Riviera between Cannes and Menton. I found Crow sitting alone at an outdoor table under the awning of a favorite restaurant called the Key Largo, facing the first row of fancy yachts.

Crow was wearing a Hawaiian sport shirt, tattered U.S. Army surplus pants, stylish sandals of soft Florentine leather, and a fisherman's cap that said, "I Hate Miami." He had recently turned forty, but he still looked much the same as when I'd first known him in his twenties. A stocky redhead with a galaxy of freckles spattered across a quizzical, blunt-featured face. He was slouched in his chair nursing a scotch on the rocks and frowning at nothing, like someone talking to himself without moving his lips.

He brightened when he saw me. "Well, well. Pete Sawyer's back in town."

I sat down beside him. "In person."

"About time, buddy. I tried to call you a few weeks ago. Wanted to bend a friendly but uninvolved ear with some things I had on my mind."

"Here I am. Friendly as ever. Uninvolved in what?"

Crow stole a glance at his watch. "I'm not in the mood right now. Another time."

"Sure."

The Key Largo's owner, Jean-Claude, came out and shook my hand. I ordered a Campari and Perrier. Crow finished off his scotch and asked for a refill. Jean-Claude went back inside, past the life-size, full-figure picture of Humphrey Bogart, standing there with his gun and a world-weary expression.

The Riviera has gotten hooked on the old Bogart image lately. There's the African Queen next door to the Key Largo, and Sam's Place in Monte Carlo, and half a dozen other spots where you can drink or dine under his sleepy, cynical scowl.

Crow was gazing at the yachts as if he'd been studying the picture and practicing that look.

"Waiting for Nathalie?" I asked him.

He shook his head. "She's in Paris. Flew up a couple days ago. Decided she wanted to confer with some department store fashion directors and merchandise managers."

"On a weekend?"

He shrugged.

I kept it casual. "When's she due back?"

"I don't know," Crow said carelessly. "Depends."

He didn't sound as if there was anything about his wife's departure, or his not knowing when she would come back, that troubled him.

But then, Frank Crowley was a deceptive guy in many ways. For example, like a lot of short people, he was packed with more energy per inch than most of us—but most of the time he didn't look it. Any more than he looked like he had the physical strength to carry somebody my size two and a half miles across rough terrain under unfriendly fire.

Maybe he'd put me down a lot. He never explained how he'd accomplished it, and I didn't know, because I'd been unconscious the whole way. I knew it was two and a half miles because that was the distance between where I'd taken the grenade burst and the forward medic tent where I came to a long time later. I knew it was Crow who'd done it because one of the medics told me he'd brought me in slung over his shoulders. And that he'd passed out from exhaustion after setting me down.

Later I'd gotten a chance to ask Crow why he'd done it. He didn't say that I'd have done the same for him, because neither of us knew if that was true. You don't know what you'll do in combat situations until you find yourself doing it.

What Crow did tell me was, "Hell, it was getting too damn grisly up there where you got clobbered. Taking you back was my only excuse for getting myself the hell out of there. Even got myself a couple days R and R in a nice comfortable tent while they were sewing you back together. Until they caught on I was malingering. You were still sleeping it off when they kicked me out."

Sacré Crow. As slang, *sacré* can signify either magnificent or damn-fool. In Crow's case, both.

Jean-Claude sent a waiter out with our drinks. We clinked glasses. Just the feel of the frosty glass against my palm was a pleasure. Even in the shade of the awning the midday heat was enervating, down there at sea level. Later there'd be the relief of the updraft between sea and mountains. But right then there wasn't a hint of a breeze, and the hot air felt almost solid. I squeezed the glass in my hand, tinkled the ice cubes inside, and took a swallow, relishing the cold sliding down my throat.

I said, "I hear you sold out your half of the business."

Crow nodded. "Who'd you hear it from?"

"Mona."

He grinned crookedly. "She thinks I've gone crazy. And she's done her best to persuade Nathalie of it."

"Your wife has a tough mind of her own. I've seen her tell Mona to butt out of her affairs a number of times.

About as rough as you can get." I smiled at a memory. "Even when she was a kid she could make her mother back off when she dug in her heels."

"In this case she seems to agree with Mona. I tried my best to explain my reasons. They're really very simple ones. So simple Nathalie can't believe it's that simple. She's sure there has to be something deeper and darker behind what I tell her."

"Try me," I said.

He looked at his watch again, and then toward the parking area. Whoever he was expecting wasn't in sight. He drank some more of his iced scotch. "I was sitting outside a café in Nice one afternoon. On the Promenade des Anglais. Reading my *Herald Tribune*, at first. Then just watching all the pretty people going by on their way to and from the beach. You know, this area has some of the best looking people in the world. Must be the mixture of French and Italian blood."

I nodded agreement. "Nathalie's one of the best-looking examples."

"That's for sure. Well, I suddenly realized that I'd been sitting there doing nothing constructive for almost two hours, and that I'd better get back to the office. Back to all the problems that never end when you're running a company like that."

He paused and squinted at me, looking for signs that I was tuned in. I gave him one of my understanding looks.

He continued to study me when he spoke again. "And then I thought—*why?* I mean, *why* did I have to go back to that pressure cooker? With all those decisions to be made? And all those employees waiting for me to make the right ones? Hell, it was getting to the point where that's all I ever thought about. Constant anxiety—nights, weekends. Even my dreams were full of it. That's why I rented that space in Nice a year ago and turned it into a photo-graphy studio and darkroom. I know everybody figured I was overindulging myself, putting that much dough into what's supposed to be just a hobby.''

"Not me.'' I gestured at the rows of yachts. "Look at all the people sinking fortunes into these boats, and most of them not using them more than a few weeks a year. They can afford it, so nobody thinks it's weird.''

"That's the point. I can afford it. That's what hit me that day on the Promenade des Anglais. That if I didn't go back to the office I'd still have a roof over my head and wouldn't go hungry. So I went to my studio instead. Spent the rest of the day cropping and blowing up pictures I'd taken of some little forgotten villages up in the mountains that tourists never get to. I didn't finish until midnight—feeling tired but *great*. From doing work that was purpose-ful and at the same time enjoyable. So I decided. Sell my half of the company and get enough out of it to last me comfortably for the next ten years. And by then maybe I can build my hobby into my new profession. A more easy-going one that won't give me ulcers.''

"Makes sense to me,'' I told him.

"I figured it would,'' Crow said. "I've heard *you* talk about quitting the detective business to start your own vine-yard.''

"If and when I get a big enough chunk of money to-gether. So far I haven't, so we can't be sure if I'd really do it. You *do* have the money. And you earned it. You're entitled to take your shot.''

Crow sighed and sipped his scotch. "I wish everybody else saw it that way. Especially Nathalie.''

"You've got to give her time to adjust to the new you, Crow. She thought she was married to a genuine American powerhouse. Nathalie's something of a powerhouse herself. What you call anxieties she regards as challenges. She likes taking them on. She thought you did, too.''

''I did. I don't anymore. My change of life, I guess. It began to get to me when I saw my fortieth birthday coming. Half my life over with. At least half. And what I was doing wasn't fun anymore. Just increasing amounts of obsessive worries. I want to spend whatever's left of my life doing something that challenges without putting that kind of strain on me.''

I smiled at Crow. ''In one American's immortal words: Go for it.''

He smiled back. ''At least I've got you and Rocky in my corner.''

''You've got Gilles, too. He was trying to calm Mona down this morning. He understands what you're doing.''

''I know. Couldn't have a better brother-in-law than Gilles. After you, my favorite guy.''

He meant it. But I got a feeling that the subject of Gilles made him uneasy for some reason. Moments later I knew why.

Crow looked again toward the parking area, and this time he saw the person he was expecting.

She came toward us wearing a Mona Vaillant design—a short, semifitted jacket over a billowing cotton peasant skirt, her honey-colored hair upswept to show all of a face that was still as breathtaking as when she'd been a top fashion model in her early twenties.

It was Gilles's wife, Anne-Marie. A long way from Antibes, where Gilles thought she was spending the day sailing with some friends.

She was surprised to see me there with Crow. But she recovered quickly and kissed me. When I kissed her back she pulled away with a mocking shake of her head. "Don't advertise if you're not selling."

It was a joke that went back a long way between us. She kissed Crow next, but only on the cheek. Maybe because I was there.

Anne-Marie had been single and making a fortune as a model when I'd gotten to know her in Paris. We had a torrid but short-lived affair that simmered down to an easy friendship. When she learned I knew Mona Vaillant she asked for an introduction. Anne-Marie had been taking art and design courses between her modeling assignments. She knew she couldn't expect to live off her looks forever.

I arranged for her to meet Mona and the rest of the family. We had begun to think Gilles was destined to be a lifelong bachelor when Anne-Marie stepped into his life. She dropped modeling for marriage and an apprenticeship in the Mona Vaillant atelier. Being Gilles's wife helped, naturally. But without real talent she would never have worked her way up to being Mona's assistant designer.

The romance between Gilles and Anne-Marie had cooled off somewhere along the line. I thought I knew what the problem was, but there was nothing anyone could say or do to cure it. If it wasn't for their son, Alain, they would probably have split by now. They were both crazy about the kid, and neither wanted to get shunted into becoming a part-time parent.

If Gilles had a mistress or occasional lovers, he handled it with extreme discretion. I was sure Anne-Marie hadn't turned celibate; and from what she'd told me a year before, there wasn't much—if any—sexual pull left in their relationship. That was the night she'd made a pass at me—half clowning, semiserious.

I had fielded it as entirely clowning: "What kind of man would go to bed with his friend's wife?"

She had given me an exasperated smile. "A Frenchman. But I keep forgetting, you're only half French. That American puritan streak keeps butting in to spoil things."

I hadn't seen much of her in the year since.

Crow asked what she'd like to drink before lunch.

"Nothing," she told him. "I've had a few already. On an empty stomach. I should get some food inside me before I have any more."

Crow called to Jean-Claude to send out menus. Anne-Marie glanced at me uncertainly, obviously worried that I intended to lunch with them. I stood up and said I had a date. I have been known to lie when the occasion demands.

Anne-Marie blew me a farewell kiss. Crow said, "Don't disappear on me again, buddy. I could use more of that friendly ear."

"I'll be in touch," I promised.

They both looked relieved to see me go. I couldn't be sure of what was going on. But judging by surface impressions, Mona Vaillant's family seemed to be unraveling and reknotting itself in complex ways, faster than I could keep up with.

It disturbed me. Hindsight later told me that it should have disturbed me a great deal more.

But even in retrospect, there wasn't anything I'd learned in Beaulieu—nor earlier in Monte Carlo—that could have prepared me for what I found late that night in the bedroom of Crow and Nathalie's house.

From Beaulieu I drove back east above the coast, stopping off at Eze-sur-Mer for lunch and then returning to my house and the repair job on the faulty water-tank valve in the attic. The job took a couple hours, and I still wasn't sure how long the repair would hold before I'd have to install a new valve. When I finally climbed down the ladder

from the attic I was grimy and dripping a couple pounds'
worth of sweat. I scrubbed the worst of the grime from my
hands and face and went for my swim.

I got to it later than I'd originally planned. The sun was
lowering, and the late afternoon breeze had begun to blow.
But in midsummer that didn't matter. The sea was still
warm, with a little surface mist stirring. The water wouldn't
cool off enough to be uncomfortably chilly until the early
hours of next morning.

Once I was out beyond the capes that sheltered the cove
below my house there were no other swimmers. That didn't
mean I had the sea to myself. Motor yachts cruised past,
leaving oily wakes. A couple dozen tiny boats from the
sailing school in Beaulieu were out there practicing tacking
maneuvers. Further out, a big Canadair swung down from
the sky and skimmed the surface, its twin engines droning
as it scooped in a bellyfull of seawater. It lifted off slug-
gishly and flew away to dump the water on a forest fire
raging in the mountains above Menton. Minutes later another Canadair arrived to scoop up another five tons of
water.

We get a lot of those fires every dry summer. The only
way to douse them, that far back in the mountains, is with
the Canadairs. Southern France currently had a dozen of
them and badly needed more.

They kept me from going out as far as I'd intended. A
few years earlier a man had disappeared while out there
swimming. The law firm of Henri and Joelle Bonnet had
engaged me to investigate his family's claim that he'd been
scooped up by a Canadair and then dropped with the water
on a fire—drowned in the belly of the plane and then burned
up. The body was never found, I didn't come across anything to substantiate the claim, and the Bonnets persuaded
the family to drop the case.

I swam back to the cove and climbed to the house feeling refreshed and pleasantly fatigued, all inner tensions temporarily drained away. After showering and getting into jeans and a sport shirt I drove up to Roquebrune, where Jules and Anne Cardinal had invited me to share their Sunday dinner.

The atmosphere in their home was as pleasant as the meal. Jules and Anne remained a contented, relaxed couple, oblivious of the fact they were violating the general trend. That started me thinking again about Frank and Nathalie Crowley—and Gilles and Anne-Marie Vaillant. So when I left the Cardinals and reached the Crowleys' home I stopped—just in case Crow had more to get off his chest.

And found the house apparently empty, though the lights were on and the door was open.

And walked inside—and to the main bedroom.

The dead man sprawled naked across the bed was August Pilon.

The naked woman who had been killed trying to escape was Anne-Marie.

6

I LOOKED AT the way Anne-Marie lay there, half-curled on the carpet near the bedroom doorway. She wasn't beautiful any longer, though the inevitable deterioration had not yet begun and her face and figure were still the same. A dead person is never attractive. It is not like looking at a lifeless statue. There is a visceral revulsion you can't help experiencing at the sight of someone who has abruptly ceased to be a complicated individual personality and has become instead an emptied corpse.

It is worse when the person killed was someone you knew well. The revulsion is compounded by a jolting reminder of your own mortality and an angry refusal of some part of you to accept it.

I reviewed once more, swiftly but in detail, everything that had been said and everything I'd sensed when I had been with Crow and Anne-Marie that day. Then I went back over what had transpired after I'd seen August Pilon with Mona Vaillant: my conversation with Mona, and then with her and Gilles. I came up with a number of contradictory possibilities and hunches, but no answers. No hard facts that told me why Mona Vaillant's detective and daughter-in-law were dead.

One thing was certain: I damn well had to try to get hold of Crow and have a detailed discussion with him before the cops got involved.

I went to the living room phone and called his studio in

Nice. After ten rings without an answer I gave up. Another possibility was that Crow might be with his former business partner, Gilbert Promice. There had to be a lot of loose ends to be dealt with concerning the change of company ownership. I knew the number for the company's main office, but all I got there was an answering machine asking me to leave my name and number so my call could be answered when the firm opened for business next morning.

I decided to try Promice's home. In the middle of dialing information for his number I hung up. The light from the living room had reflected the uniforms of two gendarmes approaching across the pool patio.

I crossed the room to meet them as they reached the open sliding door. Raymond Thibaut and Jules Garnier, from La Turbie's tiny gendarmerie. I knew both. A private detective can't function unless he has friendly relations with as many cops as possible.

"I was just phoning the gendarmerie to ask for you," I said.

They weren't surprised to see me in a house they knew wasn't mine. A gendarme's job is to keep the peace in his rural area—dealing with trouble when it occurs, but also trying to prevent it. That requires being acquainted with the residents of the area and with their interrelationships. They knew I was a close friend of Crow and Nathalie.

"Are Monsieur and Madame Crowley at home?" Garnier asked me.

"No." I answered the next question before it was asked: "I was passing and saw the lights on and decided to visit them. This door was open, so I came in. The front door is unlocked, too."

Thibaut frowned as he scanned the living room behind me. He looked like he'd been wakened out of a deep sleep.

"We got a phone call. A man who wouldn't give his name. Said he doesn't want to get mixed into other people's troubles. He claimed he was out walking his dog and heard gunshots from this house."

Garnier said, "But we do have our share of false alarm callers. This could be one of them, making the whole thing up."

"Not about the shots," I said, and I led them to the main bedroom.

They took a long look at the bodies but did not move to touch them.

Garnier asked me, "Do you know who they are?"

"Anne-Marie Vaillant and August Pilon." I explained who they were but couldn't explain what they were doing in the Crowley house together, alive or dead. I was still working on that question myself.

Thibaut grimaced. "It's going to be a fat mess. We'll have half the detectives of the region on top of us."

Garnier studied the bodies again and then looked back at me. "How long have you been here?"

"Only a few minutes. Before that I spent about three hours at the house of a couple friends. Jules and Anne Cardinal. They live close to Roquebrune, raise flowers there for the wholesale market in Nice. They'll confirm how long I was with them and when I left."

Garnier and Thibaut took me back into the living room. Thibaut used the phone there to make two calls.

One was to the gendarmerie in Roquebrune, asking them to check me out with the Cardinals.

His other call was to the Gendarmerie Nationale's regional headquarters, to report the double murder to its commanding officer. Thibault was instructed to hold me, stay put without touching anything, and wait for the team of investigators that would arrive shortly to take over.

That was what Thibaut and Garnier had expected and hoped to be told. The La Turbie gendarmerie consisted of a total of only four men, none of whom had the training to carry out a murder investigation.

I waited with them, remembering the Anne-Marie I'd known when we'd first met in Paris—before she'd come down here and I'd introduced her into the Vaillant family. I tried not to think of her as she looked now, lying empty on the floor in the other room.

7

IT WAS ALMOST two in the morning when I was taken to Nice for a formal interrogation. But not to the headquarters of the Gendarmerie Nationale.

Its Commandant had sent his Brigade de Recherche team to La Turbie: doctor, photographer, ballistics expert, fingerprint technicians, and a pair of detectives experienced in homicide cases. But at the same time the Commandant had, as required by law, notified the Procureur de la République of the La Turbie murders.

A Procureur is in charge of all public prosecutions. His first duty, on being notified of a crime, is to assign a *juge d'instruction*—an examining magistrate—to supervise the investigation. A *juge d'instruction* doesn't take part in any trial. He is in charge of the case beforehand, from the very start, with a combination of powers that has no equivalent in American or British law.

The police do their work under his control and turn their findings over to him. He combines these with the results of his own questioning of suspects and witnesses. He is the one who ultimately decides if someone should be charged and brought to trial. If he does so decide, those in charge of the trial usually assume the defendant must be guilty.

The *juge d'instruction* assigned to the La Turbie double murder, influenced by the fact that the case involved a

high-prestige family—as well as a former police officer—
had begun exercising his authority immediately.

Among his many powers was the right to decide which
police he wanted to handle the investigation. He'd had previous success working with Commissaire Justin of the Police Judiciare, at the Nice headquarters of the Police
Nationale. So it was Commissaire Justin who was instructed to take over this investigation. The team of gendarme specialists already at work on it were ordered to give
him their full cooperation.

The Police Nationale is a civil service, under the Interior
Ministry. The Gendarmerie Nationale is military, under the
Ministry of Defense. At their upper levels these two parallel law enforcement agencies are extremely jealous of
each other. But at lower levels their cops often work hand
in hand without a problem. In this case they would have
had no choice even if they hadn't liked doing so. The gendarmes began giving Commissaire Justin copies of their
preliminary findings. And he sent one of his Police Judiciare inspectors to bring me in for interrogation.

I didn't mind the change. The P.J. inspector was Laurent
Soumagnac. He was thirty-four, with Oriental eyes and a
long, wiry figure. A methodical detective whose careful,
pragmatic intellect I'd learned to respect. The eyes, and
perhaps the patience behind them, were from his Vietnam-
ese mother.

One reason he'd been chosen to handle my interrogation
was that he already knew a lot about me. The apartment
he shared with his wife Domiti and their daughter Charlotte
was in Cap d'Ail, the village just above my house. In the
past year we'd begun telling each other our life stories over
drinks in the Cap d'Ail cafés.

A neighbor and, if not yet exactly a friend, not an enemy, either.

But that wouldn't keep him from squeezing me as hard as he had to, if he caught me holding out on him. Which I intended to.

Laurent Soumagnac's tiny office was ten blocks from the beach, in the central commissariat of Nice. A five-story building of white stone with old-fashioned wooden shutters and a couple of big palm trees overcrowding the small garden in back. His office was on the fourth floor. Its window looked across Avenue Foch at three of Disney's dwarfs posing on top of a garden supplies shop.

Soumagnac sat me down on a hard metal chair and settled himself on its mate behind his desk. The city outside was very quiet. Nice is the fourth largest city in France and the capital of the Riviera. But at that hour all you heard was the sound of an occasional car, echoing loudly through the dark, empty streets.

I watched Soumagnac assemble three sheets of paper and two carbons and begin rolling them into his typewriter. For detectives everywhere, knowing how to type fast has become more essential than being able to shoot fast. Glancing at the other desk that filled most of the rest of the office, I asked: "Where's Ricard?" Yves Ricard was the P.J. inspector Soumagnac usually teamed with.

"Interrogating your friend, Frank Crowley."

"I didn't know you'd found him."

"Hour ago. Coming back to that photography studio of his. Said he went for a night drive up in the mountains. Where nobody saw him, naturally."

"Got any evidence it's a lie?"

Soumagnac turned his slanty eyes on me. "*I'm* supposed to be questioning *you*. Let's get at it. The basics first. Most of those I already know."

He recited aloud as he typed them: "Name of witness:

Pierre-Ange Sawyer. Occupation: private investigator. Previously: police detective in Chicago, narcotics agent of U.S. government in Washington, and European investigator for U.S. Senate. Present business address: same as home, called *La Ruyne*, on Chemin Serriers below Cap d'Ail. Also sometimes works in Paris, where keeps apartment.''

He paused and asked: ''Paris address?''

I gave it to him.

He typed it and resumed: ''Father of witness American, killed in liberation of France, 1945. Mother French, a decorated Resistance hero, now respected scholar in Paris. Making witness citizen of both France and America.''

''Wrong,'' I cut in. ''Just American.''

He looked at me, startled. ''I thought you had dual citizenship.''

''No. I was born in Spain, not France. My mother escaped across the border when the Gestapo seized most of her Resistance group. She registered me as an American citizen, in memory of my father.''

''You could easily obtain French citizenship, too, because your mother.''

''I've just never gotten around to it.''

Soumagnac nodded wisely: ''I understand. This way, if you get in trouble here, with someone like me, for example, you can always cry to the American consulate for help.''

I just smiled at him. It was true that some cops hesitated to be as rough with me as they might have otherwise, out of fear of triggering an international problem between France and the U.S. I never told any of them that my relationships with certain departments of the American government were no longer entirely cordial.

Soumagnac returned to typing the basic facts on me,

including my movements up to the moment I entered the Crowley house and found the bodies. He told me that Jules and Anne Cardinal had confirmed my statement about the time I'd spent with them the previous evening—and that I had left them only about fifteen minutes before the gendarmes discovered me in the Crowley house with the bodies.

"Of course," he added, "they could be mistaken about the exact timing involved. Or even be lying, out of friendship for you."

"Possible, but not very. That's why you're listing me as a witness, not as a suspect."

"For the moment you are only a witness, true. But that can change at any time. It depends entirely on what the *juge d'instruction* decides. Do you know him?"

"I know his name. Xavier Escorel. I've heard he's pretty young."

Soumagnac nodded. "Twenty-seven years old. Only two years out of magistrerial school. But he belongs to an important and influential family. Which explains why he has been getting the cream of the cases lately. Young—and extremely ambitious. Intends to become a Procureur de la République, and probably will. Escorel is very clever—and vicious. A real cunt."

Everything in French has a gender, from flowers to machine guns. A vagina is assigned the masculine gender, and a penis is feminine. You figure it out. I'm half-French, and I've never been able to.

"Escorel smells the kind of publicity he adores in this case," Soumagnac continued. "One victim and her relatives by marriage belong to the family of Mona Vaillant, a name known all over the world. He intends to name a guilty party as swiftly as possible. And to assemble a dossier that insures conviction."

"You said *a* guilty party," I pointed out. "Not *the* guilty party."

"That is what I said," he agreed. "I also tell you that Escorel will see to it that anyone who tries any tricks that interfere with his work will be brutally punished. So I warn you: Be *very* careful to give completely truthful answers to the questions I ask next."

He began by asking about my connections with every member of Mona's family—and for an account of my recent meetings with each of them. Plus what I knew of their interrelationships.

I pointed to the lavender-colored folder on his desk. It contained the preliminary findings and interrogations of the team sent by the Gendarmerie Nationale. "You already have my answers to those questions in there."

"I'm a slow reader," Soumagnac said. "Comes of being born in Saigon and not getting to a school in France until I was eleven. It's easier for me if you give me the answers verbally."

He probably knew by heart every word of the dossiers in the lavender folder. What he was after were any inconsistencies that might crop up during the verbal repetition of my statement. I made sure I didn't give him any.

I told him about seeing August Pilon with Mona on Sunday morning—and about Anne-Marie joining Crow for lunch. Those were facts that would almost certainly surface during questionings of Crow and Mona.

There were a number of things I didn't tell him.

One was that Gilles and his wife Anne-Marie hadn't cared much for each other anymore. Another was that I was fairly certain Anne-Marie had played around.

Nor did I mention that Mona was angry with Crow for giving up his business. Nor that Nathalie was upset enough with him to make me think her business trip to Paris was more like walking out on him.

Soumagnac sensed the areas where I was holding something back. He kept returning to those points, approaching them in different ways. But none of his attempts pried loose anything that could provoke him into getting really tough with me.

I had more practice in lying than he had in catching me at it.

"Obviously," he said, on one of his return approaches to a shaky area, "Pilon was working on something for Madame Vaillant."

"If he was, I don't know anything about it." That was close enough to the truth to get by, no matter what Mona said.

"Come on, Sawyer. What else would she be doing with him?"

"Maybe he was drumming up business. Trying to persuade her to contact him if she ever needs any kind of investigation done. Or to recommend him to other people."

"She already has a friend who is a private investigator."

"Maybe he didn't know that."

Soumagnac went through the rest of his list of questions and took down my answers. Finally, he leaned back in his chair and folded his lean arms across his chest.

"Tell me," he asked in a more informal tone, "what do *you* think Anne-Marie Vaillant and August Pilon were doing in that house? And why were they killed?"

"I haven't been thinking of much of anything else since I found them," I said. "And I haven't come up with an answer to either question."

Soumagnac smiled at me disbelievingly. "You're an experienced detective. You must have *some* ideas on it. Just between us.''

I smiled back: ''Laurent, don't practice your Oriental wiles on me. We both know that nothing I say in this office is just between us.''

He almost laughed. ''My Oriental wiles don't seem to be working too well. Perhaps I'm tired. One point: According to your statement, the Crowleys kept an emergency house key hidden under a tile at the corner of their patio. Did Anne-Marie Vaillant know about that?''

''*I* know it, so I guess she did too.''

Soumagnac nodded to himself, thinking about it. ''I'll tell you how it looks to me. First of all, that Opel Kadett in the Crowley carport belonged to August Pilon.''

''I didn't know that.''

''Now you do. And it's the only car there. So apparently he drove Anne-Marie Vaillant to the Crowley house. And she used that emergency key to let them in. They were naked when they were killed. The bed is all messed up. Obviously they were in bed together. Somebody came in and didn't like finding them that way. Somebody in love with either Anne-Marie Vaillant or August Pilon, say. That somebody had a gun and was furious enough to use it.''

''You use the words *apparently* and *obviously* too much,'' I said. ''They're just another way of saying you're only guessing. Your theory doesn't feel right, and you know it.''

Soumagnac unfolded his arms and leaned forward, his elbows on the desk, all attention. ''Tell me what you don't like about it.''

''First of all, if Anne-Marie and Pilon wanted to hop into bed together, why in hell would they pick a bed in the Crowleys' house to do it? Pilon was a bachelor with his own apartment.''

"Some people get an extra sexual thrill out of making love in odd places. Especially places where there is some danger of being caught at it."

I let that one pass for the moment. "Secondly, the way they were shot wasn't the work of someone crazy with anger. It was a neat, professional killing."

Soumagnac shook his head. "Being angry doesn't rule out knowing how to shoot straight."

"Something else was going on there," I told him flatly. "You can smell it, too."

"Now you're the one leaning on guesswork. And it's no better than mine."

The phone on his desk rang. He picked it up and listened for a time. Then he said, "Thanks. . . . No, nothing new here. I'll let you know."

He put down the phone and looked at me with genuine sympathy. "Your friend Frank Crowley owns a pistol."

"A lot of people do. Like most of them, he has a permit to keep a weapon in his house."

Soumagnac nodded. "For protection of domicile. But Monsieur Crowley's pistol is not where he says he always keeps it."

I already knew that, and I could guess the rest.

"His missing gun is a Czech-made M-27 that fires 7.65mm cartridges," Soumagnac said. "The bullets that ballistics just removed from the two bodies are that caliber."

8

"CROW DIDN'T KILL them," I told Soumagnac.

"That is what you wish to believe," he said gently.

"I *know* he didn't. Go with your own theory. That is was a passion killing. Crow didn't have any motivation for it."

"He was seeing his sister-in-law, one of the murder victims, alone. You saw them together yourself, yesterday in Beaulieu."

"Having *lunch* together. I was in a bar with Anne-Marie's husband that morning. That doesn't mean we're going to bed together. Anne-Marie and Crow were part of the same family. Friends, nothing more. He wasn't in love with her. He's too much in love with his own wife."

Laurent Soumagnac turned back to his machine and swiftly typed the gist of what I'd said. Then he said, "I'm adding your opinion of that to your statement. Though it's only that: an opinion. Colored by friendship. Are you saying that your friend never played around with other women?"

"If he did, I don't know of it. And *if* he did, it was just that: playing around. Not anything serious. The way he feels about Nathalie, he couldn't fall for anybody else."

Soumagnac typed it, but looking like he was only doing so to make me feel better.

I said, "There's another reason I know he didn't kill them. He's not the kind of man to kill anybody unless forced to. In self-defense, or to save somebody he cared for. Crow is a gentle person.''

He didn't type that. Instead he looked at me and said, "He was a combat soldier in Vietnam. With you. Are you trying to tell me he never killed anybody?"

"What somebody does in combat has no relation to how he'll act in civilian life. You know that. I've seen the way you've handled an armed thief who didn't want to be taken in. And I've seen you curl up like a worm when your wife Domiti bawls you out.''

Soumagnac actually blushed. "I won't type that up, if you don't mind. All right, I understand you want to save your friend. And there's no *proof* yet that he did do the killing. But if you don't like my theories about what happened, you'd better give me something that contradicts it.''

"All of you are too convinced that it was a passion killing to look beyond that," I told him. "Because it *looks* like a passion killing. Try thinking about what happened from a different angle. One of August Pilon's enemies. Private detectives collect a lot of those. Find one with a reason to kill him. And kill Anne-Marie because she was a witness—''

Soumagnac finished it for me, poker-faced: "As well as to make it *appear* to be a passion murder. Someone who threatened them with the gun first, to make them strip, for the same reason.''

"My theory is as good as yours," I told him.

"No, it's not. We're not all potato-heads here, you know. We *have* considered that possibility. Along with the possibility that the murderer was someone who wanted to frame Frank Crowley. Someone with a business grudge against him, for instance. But we haven't found one bit of evidence to lend credence to either possibility.''

"Are you searching for it?" I demanded.

"So far we have quite enough to do, just looking at what is *there*. And everything we've found indicates the murders are exactly what they look like." He glanced at his watch. It was after three. "I have other people to talk to," he said tiredly. "You're lucky. You can get some sleep now."

"Does that mean I can go?"

"Not yet. We have to hold you until we learn more."

"I hope your cells are at least clean."

It wasn't quite a cell he took me to. An ordinary little room. With a table, two chairs, and a camp bed. And a uniformed night-duty cop on guard behind a desk outside the door. What the room didn't have was a window, or any other means of escape.

After Soumagnac left I stripped to my underwear and stretched out on the camp bed. I lay on my back with my hands linked under my head, staring at the ceiling. Going over all the questions and possible answers.

I made myself stop that. The answers weren't in my head. They were somewhere outside, waiting to be tracked down after they let me go. I would need a clear mind for that, not an exhausted one.

I shut my eyes and worked at falling asleep. After a while I did, for some hours.

When I came to my watch had twenty minutes to go before nine A.M. Laurent Soumagnac sat at the table thumbing the lids off two plastic containers of coffee.

His voice was hoarse from fatigue. "I hope you take it black and strong."

The coffee smell helped get me off the camp bed and into the other chair. He slid one container across the table to me. I took a swallow and winced. It was more than strong: thick and bitter. But it did the job, jarring my brain fully awake.

Soumagnac attacked his own coffee with quick little sips, as if it was nasty medicine on which his life depended. His face was pinched and pale, the Asian cast of his eyes more pronounced. They were down to slits.

"I hate pulling night duty," he rasped between sips. "Now I get to go home, but I can never get a deep sleep in the daytime. *You* can go now, too," he told me, and he added, in an attempt at humor too heavy for his weariness to carry, "But I'd advise you to get dressed first. Though I admit you're a fine figure of a man. Except for those scars. Vietnam?"

"What's happened?" I asked him.

"You are no longer even a potential suspect. Merely a witness. Though you must make yourself available whenever the *juge d'instruction* wishes to question you further."

"Are you letting Frank Crowley go, too?"

"No."

"Can I talk to him?"

"No. Xavier Escorel has ordered him kept under *garde à vue*."

That meant keeping Crow under "close watch": locked up somewhere inside the commissariat whenever he wasn't being questioned. They could keep that up for forty-eight hours without formally accusing him of anything. During that time nobody got to see him except the police and *juge d'instruction*.

If Escorel decided not to let Crow go after that, he could officially charge him and put him under provisional detention—in the main prison of Nice—while the case against him was assembled. But at that point Crow's lawyer would have to be notified, be present when his status was changed, and thereafter have access to him in a prison room known as the parlour.

I said, "You've gotten more evidence against him."

"I'll be leaving in about fifteen minutes," Soumagnac said. "I hope the traffic on Boulevard Carabacel isn't jammed up by then."

I nodded that I understood. He was telling me where he would pick me up. At this point the dossier on Crow was priviledged information, for the eyes of the *juge d'instruction* only. Inspector Soumagnac wasn't going to divulge any part of it to me—not while he was still on duty inside the commissariat.

I got up and dressed. He sipped more of the lousy coffee and said, "You left your car keys on my desk."

I reached into my pocket and brought my hand out, closed around my car keys. "I wondered where I lost them," I said. He stayed there sipping as I went out and down the corridor to the office he shared with his partner, Yves Ricard.

The door to the office was shut but not locked. I opened it and stepped in. The air was thick with pungent cigarette smoke in spite of the open window. Ricard was behind his desk lighting another Gitane. He was a hefty, sandy-haired detective about the same age as Laurent Soumagnac, and he looked just as weary.

Crow was seated across the desk from him, seeming relaxed and in better condition than any of us.

Ricard told me, without surprise or excitement, "You're not supposed to be in here."

"Laurent told me I forgot my keys." I went to Soumagnac's desk, put my fist on it and raised it again with the keys dangling from my fingers.

Crow had turned in his chair to regard me with a tight smile. "I didn't have anything going with Anne-Marie," he told me, quickly but without panic. "And I didn't kill anybody."

"That makes my job easier," I said. "Who has any reason to frame you? Business, old grudge—*anything*."

"Nobody." He sounded sure of that, and he was smart enough to know whether it was true or not. "There has to be some other angle behind it."

I said, "Be careful what you tell the *juge d'instruction* when he questions you this afternoon. He's brainy and nasty."

I didn't tell him not to answer any questions without his lawyer present. In France you have to answer any questions put to you by the law, under any conditions. Refusal to answer gets marked in your dossier as evidence of guilt.

"I don't fluster too easy," Crow reminded me. "But thanks for the warning."

Yves Ricard pointed to the door. He still wasn't excited, but my unofficial visit time was up. I put a hand on Crow's shoulder and squeezed it and walked out.

Soumagnac was waiting in the corridor to escort me to the commissariat entrance.

Outside, the garden supplies shop across the street was opening for business. In daylight you could see the statues of Disney's dwarfs needed a new paint job. Dopey's smile had faded to a sinister smirk.

I walked away quickly, to make sure I'd be waiting on Boulevard Carabacel when Inspector Soumagnac got there. But I came to a halt less than thirty feet from the commissariat building.

Arlette Alfani Vallaresso was sitting outside a bistro on the corner.

She was having coffee and the last croissant from one of the little serving baskets that usually contained three or four. There was a black briefcase on the table beside her cup. She wore an open black vest over a simple tan dress.

The pockets of the vest bulged with a note pad, two pens, and a miniature cassette recorder. The dress was loose-fitting except where a slim belt cinched it at her waist, and its hem was well below her knees, even sitting down. None of it managed to make her less devastating.

She was probably brilliant at preparing cases for trial, but I doubted that she'd make an effective courtroom lawyer. No jury would take her seriously. Not until she grew older, anyway, and her metabolism stopped burning off all the food she ate.

Arlette stood up as I neared her. "I've been waiting almost an hour for you and Crowley to come out." There was no trace of the careless temptress in her voice or manner now. That was something she could switch on and off.

"How did you find out about it?" I asked her.

"Mona Vaillant called me late last night, after the police came to talk to her. She was trying to get in touch with Henri and Joelle Bonnet. But they're still off in Japan, so . . ." Arlette finished by placing a hand to her heart. She didn't look happy to have this heavy a responsibility dropped on her alone. But neither did she look frightened by it.

"I have to talk to Mona," I told her. "Soon. Where will she be this morning?"

"I can phone and find out."

"Get me an appointment with her. No later than noon."

Arlette nodded and gestured toward the commissariat. "What about Frank Crowley? The Bonnets represent him, too."

"He's been put under *garde à vue*."

She took it without flinching. "On what kind of evidence? Hard or circumstantial?"

"I'm about to find out. Meet me at my place in half an hour and I'll tell you." I started past her.

She snatched up her briefcase: "I'll come with you."

That stopped me and spun me around. Soumagnac wouldn't open up with an attorney present. I stabbed a finger at her: "*No*. I'll see you in half an hour."

Arlette registered the expression on my face. "I'll be there."

This time she stayed put when I strode away.

9

SOUMAGNAC PICKED ME up at the corner of Carabacel and Rue Devoluy. He drove across the Paillon River and turned up the Avenue of the Blue Devils, climbing toward the start of the Grande Corniche. "Your car's still up there at La Turbie," he said in that tired, draggy voice. "I'll drop you off by it."

I said, "Thanks," and I wondered if he'd get to the subject himself or if I would have to prompt him. I waited while he concentrated on maneuvering over a mountain shoulder via a narrow road that kept curling back on itself like a long strand of dropped spaghetti. That shoulder was one of the relatively uninhabited spots left around the edges of Nice. The police called it "No Man's Land" because at least one morning every year they'd find some victim of a gangland execution tossed out there—a result of sporadic warfare among Arab, Corsican, and Italian mobs for control of the area.

From up on that shoulder there was a view of all of Nice, spreading out around the Bay of Angels to the airport at the far end. The view confirmed the statistics: Nice is the fastest-growing city in France. For much the same reason as the population explosion in Florida: a warm sun luring permanent residents down from colder places up north. New construction rose over the hills behind the city and continued into the interior, like the work of hundreds of termite colonies. One moment I saw all of it, and the next moment it was gone, hidden by a hill behind the car. Then we were onto the divided highway of the Grande Corniche, with the mountains of Italy rising ahead of us beyond Menton.

I was about to prompt him when he finally spoke. What came out of him surprised me. "What do you *feel* like most," he asked, "American or French?"

I stared at him, trying to adjust to the unexpected question.

"I always wondered," he said. "Now that I know you're not even a citizen of France I wonder more."

He looked embarrassed. It was an intimate sort of question. We'd known each other a while, but we hadn't gotten into intimate feelings before. It might help. I told him, "American."

"Why? You live here."

"But I got all my schooling in America. They taught me about George Washington and the cherry tree in kindergarten. By college I knew America is the greatest nation on earth: God's country. I think it's where you go to school that matters, more than your parents' nationality."

Inspector Soumagnac thought about it and nodded to himself. "That's probably true. I was born in Saigon, and my mother's not French, but most of my schooling was here in France. Learning that France is the only truly civilized country. With the greatest philosophers, most important art, best food."

"So you feel French."

"Yes, but I live here. You do, too, but you feel American."

"America is my country," I tried to explain, "but that house below Cap d'Ail is my home. That's confusing, but there it is. I grew up spending every summer vacation there with my mother. It's in my bones."

"I never see your mother around Cap d'Ail."

"She prefers Paris. If it wasn't for me she'd probably sell the house. She's not as sentimental about it as I am."

Soumagnac nodded understandingly. "Men are the sentimental ones. Women are not. They're romantic—and not troubled by undue sentiment when one romance is over and they wish to begin another."

"Are you stating that as a fact," I asked him with some skepticism, "or just a stray notion?"

He grinned. "It is something my father always says. But he is not known in the family for exceptional brainpower. Definitely not one of the great philosophers of France."

I figured we were intimate enough by then. "What's keeping Frank Crowley under *garde à vue*?"

Soumagnac hesitated. "I'm not supposed to divulge anything about that. It's strictly classified until the *juge d'instruction* questions Crowley himself—and decides what information he wishes released to the public."

I said, "You know I'm not going to tell anybody you talked to me. And I know you don't like this *juge*."

Soumagnac made a sour face. "Xavier Escorel is too excited about this case. He's pushing us too hard—and much too fast. Grabbing at everything we give him, not allowing us enough time to sift around for other indications that might contradict what he already thinks he has. I told you—he's a big head, and an even bigger cunt."

"What *do* you have on Crow?"

"His pistol was found a few minutes before six this morning. Four bullets fired from it. Recently."

That news did not surprise me. "Where was it found?"

"Inside the water tank behind the toilet in the Crowley's guest bathroom."

I didn't bother pointing out that Crow was an intelligent

man. And that he would have had to be very dumb, if he was the one who fired the four shots, to hide the pistol where a thorough search was certain to find it. Soumagnac knew that. But he also knew that people confused by panic after such an act sometimes committed atypical stupidities.

"Ballistics will get to work with the gun this morning," he told me. "To see if bullets they fire from it match the ones found in the bodies of the two victims."

That was one thing I was sure of: They *would* match.

Soumagnac said, "Escorel has scheduled his session with your friend Crowley for two-thirty this afternoon. By then he'll have the ballistics report. Along with our dossiers."

"What else will he have?" I asked him.

"Three Polaroid photographs of Anne-Marie Vaillant that have been discovered in Frank Crowley's studio. Nudes. Extremely erotic. Your friend swore to Ricard that he never took any kind of photographs of her, but—"

"But somebody's done a neat job of framing him."

"There is no sign that anyone forced their way into his studio to leave those pictures there."

"Anybody who knows how to use the right tools could do it without leaving a trace. *I* could."

"It's a possibility," Soumagnac granted. "But without any evidence at all to support it, it's one that our *juge d'instruction* can safely ignore."

I asked him, "What's the rest of the statement your partner took from Frank Crowley?"

He recited Crow's story in a weary monotone: "He never had sexual relations with Anne-Marie Vaillant and wasn't in love with her. They never even flirted with each other. He didn't take the pictures of her that were found in his studio."

"Why were they having lunch together yesterday in Beaulieu?"

"He says she phoned him early yesterday morning and asked him to meet her. Said it was urgent. After you left them she said she knew his wife was away and asked if she could use his house that night. She wouldn't explain why, only that it was important to her. He says he figured it was for a rendezvous with some lover, and he didn't like her using his place for that. But she acted so desperate that he finally gave in and agreed. He figured he'd sleep on the couch in his studio, and it was only for one night. He didn't have to give her a key to his house. She knew where the emergency key was hidden.

"He says he was at his studio around ten o'clock last night when he got a surprise phone call from her. She told him she was up in the hills near Lucéram. Her car had conked out there, and she begged him to come up and get her. So he went."

"Making absolutely sure," I said, "that he wouldn't be able to prove where he was when she and Pilon were killed."

Soumagnac didn't respond to that one. "He says he couldn't find her near Lucéram, and he spent time driving around the area, figuring she might have given him the wrong location. But he couldn't find her, and finally he gave up. Thought maybe somebody else came along and got her car started for her. He drove back down to Nice and into the hands of a couple of cops at his studio. And that's it."

"What does he say about August Pilon?"

"That he never met him. Never even heard of him."

"Your people must have had a look in Pilon's office by now."

"There, and his apartment. He was a neat type. Detailed files on all his jobs. But nothing over the past couple of weeks."

That figured. "No messages on his answering machine?"

"None."

"Or they were erased."

"Or that," Soumagnac agreed blandly.

"What do his friends say he's been doing?"

"Pilon was between girlfriends. He didn't have any men friends. Not even from his time as a cop."

"How come?"

"He liked to play with other men's wives. Then he'd joke about it and drop them."

"A credit to the human race."

"Truly." Soumagnac didn't bother to mention that Pilon's way with other men's wives fitted his being found with Anne-Marie.

"No signs of forced entry into Pilon's office or apartment, I suppose. Same as with Crowley's studio."

"That's right," he said, without expression.

"But nothing left to show what he's done for two weeks. Peculiar, wouldn't you say?"

"*I'd* say. But you know how the gears operate. Once a *juge d'instruction* takes over a case, the police have to concentrate on searching for what *he* wants them to find."

I said, "But *I* don't. Somebody is trying to sew Crow up. And your Xavier Escorel likes that fine. Daughter-in-law of famed Mona Vaillant murdered with lover by Mona Vaillant's son-in-law. Headlines all the way. With Escorel's picture in newspapers all over Europe and America."

"Be careful," Soumagnac warned me quietly. "Escorel's family has highly placed friends. He won't like you if you break his toy."

I felt something stretch my mouth. Almost like smiling too widely, but I knew it couldn't look pleasant. "He can like it or not, Laurent. If Escorel tries to run with this frame, I'll make him *eat* it. Splinters and all.''

We were approaching La Turbie by then, in sight of the massive stone columns that loomed above it. They were all that remained of a huge monument raised by Caesar Augustus to celebrate the Roman conquest of the region. The rest of the monument collapsed in an earthquake long ago. All the older buildings of the town were built with blocks of cut stone looted from that collapse over the centuries since.

Soumagnac pulled over across the road from my car, a few feet from a bistro. I climbed out of his car and said, "Come on in and I'll buy you a double *calva*.''

He shook his head. "Thanks, but I don't drink in the morning.''

"That's your sleeping problem,'' I told him. "You think this is morning. But for you it's the end of the day. You need something to quiet your nerves.''

He was still looking dubious when he entered the bistro with me. I ordered the Calvados for him and a cup of genuine coffee for myself. As we drank I asked what Mona Vaillant had told the police.

"I don't know yet,'' he said. "Didn't have time to see their report before I went off duty.'' He finished his drink with a smile of embarrassed pleasure. "I hope this doesn't work. If it does, I'll be on my way to becoming an alcoholic by the time I stop pulling night duty.''

"Rest your mind,'' I told him. "It's healthier for you than taking a lot of sleeping pills.''

I paid and we walked outside. "Remember what I told you,'' he said, and his voice had lost its raspy sound. "Be careful about getting Escorel mad enough at you to hit back. He's the kind of guy that doesn't forget. And he's got the patience to wait for an opportunity.''

"I'll remember you warned me," I promised.

He got in his car and headed for Cap d'Ail, turning the next corner cautiously.

I crossed the road to my car and drove down toward my place—to meet Arlette and find out what Mona had told her and the police about August Pilon.

⊠ **10** ⊠

SHE WAS BEHIND the wheel of a brand new white Porsche, waiting for me outside the locked gate at the top of the private drive that led down the slope below the Lower Corniche to my house. I was one of seven householders who had keys to the gate. That was one reason the little cove at the bottom of the slope was never crowded, even in July and August. People without keys could *walk* all the way down to the beach there, but it was a long, stiff climb getting back up.

"Did you get Mona?" I asked Arlette as I got out to unlock the gate.

"No, but she's expected back at her house soon. I left word for her to call us here."

I opened the gate, and she drove through and continued along the hairpin turns of the drive. I took my Peugeot in, relocked the gate, and drove down after her past the other six houses, each screened from the others by trees and flowering bushes. My house was the last, at the bottom of the drive. An ancient, rebuilt dwelling with solid stone walls and a sloped orange-tiled roof, backed by a wide terrace flanked by fruit trees, palms, and pines. No swimming pool, but it was only a four-minute hike down a path from the terrace to the sea. The climb back up took about eight minutes, if you were in good condition.

I pulled into the carport next to Arlette's Porsche. Like the Crowleys and a lot of other rural homeowners, I kept a spare key hidden on the grounds. Arlette had already gotten it and gone inside. She was in the kitchen opening drawers and cupboards when I entered the living room. She didn't need my help. Everything was in the same general place as two years before.

The answering machine hooked to the house phone was my substitute for an office and secretary. There were only two messages on it, neither of which I was in a mood to do anything about that morning. Nothing from Mona Vaillant. I went through the bedroom to shower and shave.

I was getting into a fresh pair of Levi's and a light blue sport shirt when delicious smells from the kitchen made my stomach growl an angry reminder that I was very hungry. Putting on espadrilles, I headed for the smells. Arlette had squeezed enough oranges to fill two tall glasses, and she was already sitting down to a generous plateful of ham omelet and buttered toast. I sat down to mine. While I ate I told her everything Laurent Soumagnac had told me. *After* extracting her promise not to reveal where I'd gotten it.

She listened to all of it without interposing questions. I could almost see the mind behind those attentive eyes going to work on the information, sorting, calculating, rearranging, evaluating.

When I finished my recital and breakfast I got up to brew some herb tea. Arlette noted which herbs I selected without comment. She was accustomed to men remembering what she liked.

"Your turn," I said. "What did Mona tell the police?"

"That she hired August Pilon to check into whether someone might be stealing the designs for her collections and passing them to competitors. No specific competitors—

it was just a possibility that began worrying her. Yesterday morning Pilon told her he was making progress. Expected to soon be able to tell her if her suspicion was justified or not. But he didn't tell her anything specific, and she's not sure if he really had any information. *And* she has no idea what he was doing with Anne-Marie in the Crowleys' home. Dressed or undressed.''

"Alive or dead," I added, and I set Arlette's tea on the table. I poured myself a cold glass of milk and sat down across from her. "Now," I said, "that's what Mona told the police. What did she tell *you*?"

"Pretty much the same. Except for some things I already knew. Such as the name of the Paris designer who got the advance information about her last collection. Mona came to Henri and Joelle Bonnet with the problem. They recommended you first, of course. But she said there was a reason in this case why she preferred not to use you. She wouldn't explain why, but she was determined on that point. So the Bonnets suggested she try August Pilon.''

"Did he ever report back to the Bonnets about how he was approaching the job?''

"No. And neither did Mona. She—''

At that moment my phone rang. I was in the living room picking it up after the second ring. It was Mona.

"I'm back home now," she told me. Her voice was strained, but it was a strain she had under control. "At noon I have a business lunch I can't get out of, and after that several vital meetings. But if you can get here soon—''

"I'm on my way," I told her, and I hung up.

"The fashion house that stole my designs," Mona told me, "is Lotis. I'm sure you know of it.''

I did. Serge Lotis, who had founded the company and who remained its president and head designer, had been a big name in fashion longer than Mona Vaillant. "Why would he have to steal from you?" I asked her. "His own designs have always done big business."

"They used to. But Serge Lotis has lost his touch. Over the past three years his collections haven't been well received."

Mona looked like she hadn't had any more sleep than I had. The lines around her eyes and mouth were deeper than usual. But her voice was steady enough, though the undercurrent of strain came through. "You know how fickle the market is. How much the success of a fashion house depends on an ability to spot changing trends far in advance."

She'd lectured me on it in the past. Her profession was in large part a matter of long-range guesswork. When a fashion house showed a collection it was predicting what women would want to wear six to eight months later. People like Mona and Lotis began preparing designs for a collection almost a year before their clothes would actually be competing for sales in the retail stores.

"You're saying Lotis's crystal ball has cracked."

"That's one way of putting it," Mona said. "He's been trying to recapture interest by resorting to wilder and wilder styles. Clothes that only a teenager could get by in. Young girls look good in anything. Adult women don't—and they haven't been buying his lines."

We were out on the veranda of Mona's home, she and I in deck chairs and Arlette standing against one of the pillars, arms folded on her breast, watching us and listening, alert to every nuance.

The house was one of the turn-of-the-century mansions on the outskirts of Nice, on the slopes of Mont Boron. A wealthy enclave where the old rich were slowly giving way to the new rich like Mona Vaillant. A high stone wall surrounded her property, enclosing a large lawn and garden and a gatehouse in addition to the main house. A Spanish couple who had worked for her almost ten years lived in the gatehouse. The wife did the housekeeping and cooking. The husband took care of the grounds and maintenance, as well as sometimes acting as her chauffeur.

The big house was Victorian: dark brick walls, gables and turrets and bay windows, four chimneys connected to separate fireplaces. Half the ground floor space inside had been converted into a multiroomed atelier for Mona.

Every successful fashion house has its own way of functioning. The headquarters of Mona Vaillant's business was in a building in the middle of Nice, where there were also workshops for the women who made her patterns and first samples and room for the storage of materials. The factory that manufactured her clothing was on the other side of town. But the atelier where Mona created her final designs was in her home.

The veranda where we were meeting was outside a part of her atelier that she called her Nightmare Room. That was where she kept a rack on which were hung past creations of hers that had failed to sell. There weren't that many garments on that rack, but Mona always said it was a humbling, salutary experience to look at them whenever she began feeling too full of herself. She didn't look full of herself at the moment.

"There have been rumors," Mona told me, "that Lotis was financially overextended and in danger of going under. But then he brought out his new Haute Couture collection. At the beginning of July, three weeks before any of the other fashion houses were to show theirs. It was *very* well received.'' Her tone had gotten bitter. "The orders poured in."

"And his designs were yours."

"Almost all. Slightly altered, of course. Just enough to get away with it, according to the Bonnets."

"In fashion," Arlette told me quietly, "plagiarism is almost impossible to prove. I guess that's not news to you. *That's* why the Bonnets warned her not to make any claims against Serge Lotis. He *could* sue her for slander. And possibly win. How do you prove which designer thought up an idea first?"

Mona was having increasing difficulty containing her anger. "I had to scrap my own Couture show. People would have said *I* was copying from *him*. That meant a hard loss of income and big expenses. The firm can survive that this time. I'd only prepared thirty-two garments for that collection. But *now* I'm preparing for one of my two biggest shows of the year."

"In October," I said. "Your ready-to-wear collection for next spring and summer."

"I'll have prepared over a hundred and seventy different garments for that show," Mona told me. "If Serge Lotis gets hold of *those* in advance . . ."

It was time for me to explain something to Arlette. "She didn't hire *me* to find out how Lotis has been getting her designs because she thinks the source is inside her family."

Mona had tried unsuccessfully to stop me. Now she was glaring. "I told you that in *confidence*. I didn't—"

I let an edge of irritation into my voice. "Mona, Arlette is your attorney. She has to know what's going on. It's not just the theft of your work we're dealing with now. Crow is in jail, and two people are dead."

I watched the bitter anger drain out of her, leaving her

suddenly older. She leaned back in her chair and closed her eyes, as though in pain. "I know it's stupid to blame myself, but . . ."

She opened her eyes, but not all the way, squinting as though the sunlight bothered them. But the veranda was well shaded against the sun. "I'm the one who hired Pilon. He must have questioned Anne-Marie—though he didn't tell me so, and I had asked him not to talk to anyone in my family about it. So I'm responsible for Anne-Marie's meeting him. And she was . . . vulnerable to men, as you know."

"Did *Gilles* know that, too?" I asked Mona.

"If he did, he never mentioned it to me. He's always been so secretive about his deeper feelings. But I don't think he cared much for her anymore. *I* cared more. Not only because she is the mother of my grandson. Because of her talent as well. She had become almost indispensable to my work."

Arlette suddenly spoke up again, quietly. "Let's get back to the important point, Mona. *Why* does Serge Lotis's source have to be one of your family?"

"Nobody else *knew* my entire Couture line. Not early enough for Lotis to use it when he did. I thought so before Pilon flew to Paris to check. What he reported confirmed it: Lotis began working on his variations on my styles well before I had them all ready for the factory."

I asked her, "Did Pilon talk to Serge Lotis himself?"

"I warned him not to—because of what Henri and Joelle Bonnet said. About not stirring Lotis to retaliation. Pilon did talk to somebody who worked for Lotis, though he wouldn't give me the name. He also told me he was very close to getting me the name of the traitor who gave Lotis my designs. But I'm not sure if that was the truth, or only something he was saying to keep me paying him. Now we'll never know.''

"When did Pilon get back from Paris?"

"Late Saturday night. He phoned me, and we met Sunday morning—when you saw us together. If he was telling me the truth, the timing of the preparation of the Lotis Haute Couture collection doesn't leave any doubt. Only four people could have given Lotis all the designs: Gilles, Nathalie, Crow, or Anne-Marie.''

Arlette said, "You have other assistant designers besides Anne-Marie. They must have known your collection, too.''

Mona shook her head. "They work for me on a freelance basis. I call them contributing designers, rather than assistants. I take similar precautions with them as with my other workers: the pattern makers, fitting models, seamstresses, tailors, fabric buyers. Each contributing designer knows only those few designs he or she actually works on. Either from preliminary ideas I suggest or ones of their own. They bring what they've done to me, and I make the final modifications on any I decide to go with.''

I said, "So the only designer besides yourself who knew all of the line you'd decided on was Anne-Marie.''

"That's right. She made detailed sketches of everything for me to work with. And she took part in my conferences with Gilles and Nathalie. During the planning of a collection and when we were working out the publicity and selling campaigns for it.''

"You implied," Arlette reminded her, "that Frank Crowley also had access to all your designs.''

"In this case, yes. I asked him to photograph the Couture line while I was still working on it. To see if photos would be more helpful than the sketches in giving me any final inspirations. They weren't.'' Mona glanced at me nervously. "But Crow *could* have kept copies of his pictures.''

"Anyone who could get into your atelier could have taken pictures of your designs,'' I told her. "The couple who work for you, for example.''

"No. When I'm not actually working with design I keep it in a windowless room with an alarm system and a Chubb combination lock on the door. I'm the only one who knows the combination.''

I didn't bother explaining the ways that difficulty could be dealt with by someone determined enough. But it *would* be simpler just to get to someone who knew the designs. And that did narrow down the possibilities. "I'll have to talk to Gilles and Nathalie,'' I said. "Where are they?''

"Nathalie is on her way back from Paris. I phoned her hotel there last night after the police came, but she wasn't in. She was staying the night with friends outside the city, but I didn't know that. I left a message, and she phoned me when she returned to the hotel this morning.''

"And Gilles?''

The answer surprised me. "He's on his way to Australia. We're considering opening our first boutique there. He left last night.'' Mona looked at her watch. "He should be landing about now. I've left a message at his hotel for him to phone me immediately.''

Arlette told her, "He'll know what's happened before he gets your message. The French police will have alerted the Australian police. They'll be waiting at the airport to talk to him when his plane comes in.''

"In either case,'' Mona said, "I'm sure Gilles will take the first return flight he can get a seat on. But even so, he can't get back before tomorrow.''

I asked her, ''When did his flight to Australia take off?''

''At nine-thirty last night.''

That left Gilles out as a suspect. He'd been in the air when his wife and Pilon were murdered.

It did not, however, erase the possibility of his having a hired professional do it while he was gone.

I didn't believe Gilles would do something like that. But I didn't think Crow had killed them, either. And somebody had.

⊠ 11 ⊠

"LET'S ESTABLISH ONE thing," Arlette said after we left Mona and walked back to our parked cars. "Who do you represent in this mess—Mona Vaillant or Frank Crowley?"

"Crow."

"Has he formally retained you to do so?"

"He doesn't have to. The Bonnet firm gets a yearly retainer to handle all his problems. Right now you're the Bonnet firm. You're going to retain me to work on Crow's defense, because that's what Henri and Joelle Bonnet would do."

Arlette considered it. "Makes sense. That will be interesting. I've never worked with you before." She looked at her watch as we reached the cars. "I have to get to the office. There are several other cases I'm preparing for the Bonnets. They'll have to be put on delay for the moment, so I can deal with this one. I want to be ready by the time the *juge d'instruction* sees Crowley this afternoon."

"If Xavier Escorel decides to press charges, he'll have to finally let you talk to Crow." That didn't mean *I'd* get a chance to talk to him. Nobody talked to a charged prisoner except his attorney and very close family. "If so, I'll want to know everything he tells you."

Arlette nodded. "We'll have to keep in close touch every day on anything either of us learns. I'd suggest you try finding out about August Pilon's recent movements, here and in Paris. In spite of what Inspector Soumagnac told you, Pilon might have left some trace of—"

"Don't teach your grandmother to suck eggs," I told her.

"What?"

"Ancient saying. It means I was doing this kind of work, and figuring out where the likeliest leads might be, while you were still in diapers."

She said evenly, "Yes, but with doddering senility so close you may be forgetting how."

"Cruelty," I told her, "is not one of the qualities I admire in a lady."

"Truce? Or do we go on kicking each other?"

"Truce. But *you* check on August Pilon. You're the lawyer, and he worked for lawyers. Call around, see if any of them know anybody he was intimate with that the cops missed. I'm going to be busy looking into other corners."

"All right. I'll talk to Crowley's partner, too. He's our client, and I know him. Right now he's in New York, but he'll be home tomorrow night."

"Fine." After I heard what he told her I could decide if I should do any further digging into Crow's partner myself.

"Don't forget," Arlette said, "we exchange information. Regularly. The Bonnets will be back in a week. I want to have as much as possible already prepared for the defense. Even though it can't come to trial for months, no matter how Escorel pushes it."

"Crow's not going on trial," I told her, and realized my voice was harsher than I'd intended. "I'm not going to let him sit in prison, waiting for it to come to that."

I stopped off at the first post office inside Nice and put through a long-distance call to Fritz Donhoff in Paris.

Fritz and I had worked as partners for some years up

there. I still had my apartment next door to his, and we still sometimes worked together when a case brought him to the Riviera or me to Paris. Though an unshakably old-fashioned man in most ways, he'd learned that an answering machine in his apartment did avoid a lot of unnecessary office expenses. But it was his own heavy, melodious voice I got on the line after the third ring.

"I'm glad I caught you in," I told him.

"I won't be going out for a week or two," Fritz said. "I slipped off a curb and broke some blood vessels in my ankle. Embarrassing. It's swollen and blue, and I have to stay put with my leg up most of the time."

"Jesus, Fritz, when will you learn to be more careful? At your age things like that take a long time to heal. Have you hired someone to take care of you?"

"No need to get so upset, Peter," he said in a calming tone. "It is a small injury, though annoying. And no need to hire anyone. A number of the local ladies are taking turns looking after me."

I relaxed. If his "local ladies" were on the job, there was nothing to worry about. Fritz was seventy-three, and he'd spent all those years learning a lot more than I knew. One of the things he'd learned best was the usefulness of old-world charm. His only problem would be preventing the women from fighting over which of them should take care of him most.

I told him everything that had happened, in detail. From when I'd seen August Pilon with Mona Vaillant the previous morning to the moment of my calling him. Being stuck in his apartment wouldn't prevent him from working for me. Fritz had been operating in Paris since 1938. His network of official contacts, useful friends, people who owed him favors, and others whose vulnerable spots he knew was staggering. He could accomplish more with a

telephone than most detectives could with a full staff of
investigators out on the prowl.

I didn't tell him what I needed from him. Fritz would
figure that out as he went along. He'd do what I was going
to do: fumble around through all the unknowns until something of interest cropped up.

"Someone close to Serge Lotis is bound to be vulnerable
to judiciously applied pressure," Fritz said. "Perhaps several someones. When I find out which ones I'll invite them
here for a talk. And I'll try to get a line on Pilon's movements in Paris."

"Another possibility," I said. "When I first knew Anne-
Marie she was already into big fees as a magazine model.
But before that she worked as a clotheshorse for different
fashion houses. I don't know which ones."

"Interesting possibility," Fritz agreed. "And simple to
check. We'll see if she and Lotis knew each other."

"If you come across a solid lead that requires legwork,
let me know and I'll get up there."

"It is always a pleasure to see you, my boy."

I left the post office and went to see if I could break into
Gilles's and Anne-Marie's apartment.

Nice is a seaside resort that grew into a genuine city
with a bustling life independent of tourism. The resort is
still there and still flourishing. It extends for several miles
along the Promenade des Anglais, where the luxury hotels
look across at the beaches. But it is only a few blocks deep.
Behind it is the Nice of the permanent residents, with its
industries and university and vast urban sprawl. The apartment house was in the heart of the city on Rue Rossini, on
a quietly expensive block of solid, dignified stone buildings
equally remote from the tourist strip and the urban sprawl.

City dwellers are not like country people, even in the

sun-lulled ambience of the Côte d'Azur. They don't leave spare keys outside their apartments. And I didn't have the state-of-the-art burglar's tools I'd spoken to Soumagnac about. But what I did have, taken from my car, would probably suffice in this case.

One big advantage was knowing the interior layout of the apartment, from my visits as an invited guest. That included remembering what the door and window locks were like. You pay attention to those details automatically when you've been a cop.

I left my car at the end of the block and considered the layout as I approached the five-story building. Their apartment took up the two bottom floors. Big rooms, high ceilings, spacious closets and corridors, lots of nooks and crannies. The place had been built in the days when architects believed that people deserved decent amounts of breathing space around them. The ground floor contained the living room, dining room, kitchen, and storage space, in addition to a workroom for Anne-Marie and a study-cum-office for Gilles. Upstairs was the master bedroom suite, separated by a library from their small son's bedroom and playroom, and accommodations for the Irish nanny who looked after Alain when his parents were working.

I pressed the button beside the building's entrance, activating a buzzer and a click as the door unlocked itself. I stepped into the building's small entry and shut the door behind me.

The buzzer was there to alert a concierge, who would come up out of the basement to make sure you had a right to be in the building. But few buildings in France have concierges any more. They were phased out, along with a number of other old traditions, around the time the French decided Elvis Presley was the most significant American cultural export since Edgar Allen Poe. Only the buzzer system of entry remains, a leftover from the old days and a means of entering almost any building without being questioned.

That didn't get me into their apartment, however. The entry hall contained a cage elevator and spiral staircase, both leading to the top floor. I went around them to the apartment door.

There was no reason anyone should be in the apartment. Monday wasn't one of the maid's two days a week to come in and clean. The nanny would be taking her vacation in Dublin while Alain spent the summer with his grandparents in the mountains. Gilles wasn't back from Australia, and Anne-Marie would never be back. The police were unlikely to have gone to the trouble to obtain a warrant to enter for a look around. They would wait until Gilles returned and ask him to let them in. That wouldn't be a priority in their investigation.

Just to make sure, I rang the bell. No response. Good. I tried the door. Locked solid. Two locks. I remembered them. Not something I could deal with unless I was ready to make a lot of noise and take a lot of time.

Beyond the apartment door, at the rear of the entry hall, was another door that led out to a back garden shared by the building's tenants. It, too, was locked. But the lock was much simpler than the ones on the apartment door.

I took from my pocket a short, thin steel pick with a small wooden grip. It got the lock open quickly, but not silently. Hoping none of the tenants was in the back garden, I opened the door and stepped out. The garden was empty. There was a long rose trellis screening the tall French windows along the rear wall of the apartment. I walked between the trellis and the wall until I reached the last set of windows, outside the living room. There the side wall of the next building jutted out a few feet. That and the trellis together afforded a certain amount of conceal-ment from anyone gazing down from the backs of other buildings.

None of the windows of the apartment had bars covering them. The sturdy locking system on the apartment's door was Gilles's only concession to the insurance company. He knew an experienced, well-equipped thief could get through any defense, given time. The only way to stop worrying about it, Gilles figured, was to keep everything really val-uable locked away in a bank vault. Sensible of him. But I was after information, not valuables.

What did cover the windows were stout louvered shut-ters. Closed and locked. Louvered shutters don't present a problem, if you know how and where they're locked inside. I got out a bent wire: thick and stiff. Crouching, I slid it down through one of the lowest louver openings, at exactly the right spot. When I had it hooked under the latch I yanked up. The latch sprang free from its socket. I straightened up and did the same thing to the top latch.

If the glass doors inside were locked I was prepared to handle that with a combination of wire and prick, plus a knife blade. But it wasn't necessary. As I'd hoped, the glass doors had been left wide open so air coming through the louvers could circulate through the apartment. Arti-ficial air conditioning has never gained much favor in France.

I opened the shutters just enough to slip inside the living room. Then I stopped and stared.

All the drawers in the room had been pulled out and set on the carpet. Their contents were spread neatly around them. The closets were wide open. So were the doors of the small corner bar.

Somebody had been there before me.

Somebody was still there. Braced against the wall just behind me.

A heavy fist with power behind it thudded against the back of my ear and drove me to the floor.

⊠ **12** ⊠

I EXECUTED A fast roll the instant I hit the floor and came up on one knee with my hands cocked to strike back, ready to spring the rest of the way up in whatever direction proved best.

What proved best was that I not move another inch.

His hands were broad, with thick, short fingers. Soiled white cotton work gloves made them thicker. His left hand was still clenched in a fist. His right was aiming a snub-barreled revolver at my face. It looked like a .357 Colt Python. That close to my eyes the muzzle was huge. Not as wide as a cannon nor as deep as a grave, but sufficiently depressing.

I stayed on one knee with my other foot braced against the floor, ready to make my try anyway if I saw that gloved finger begin to tighten on the trigger.

The finger waited. He looked down at me, and I looked up at him.

He wore a long zipped-up brown nylon jacket, baggy dungarees, and black jogging shoes. He was as big as me, but most of his height was in his torso. His legs were short. The jacket fitted loosely, except where his shoulders bulged the material.

His face was hidden by a ski mask that covered all of his head. There wasn't enough light coming through the louvered shutters to see anything behind the mask's eyeslits except dark holes.

"There are people in the street outside," I said. "And more behind those open windows across the garden. And a cop car cruising around the block. That gun will make a very loud noise. If you try to put me out any other way, I'll fight, and you'll have to shoot and make that noise."

I didn't know how much of the rest of it he believed, but the noise part had to bother him. He had probably already been considering that. It would account for my still being alive and talking. Instead of dead and no further trouble to him.

It was also possible, of course, that my presence didn't trouble him at all. From the way I'd come in he had to figure I was just a burglar. A fellow professional with a different purpose. That might amuse him.

Backing up a step, he unclenched his left hand and gestured with it for me to stand up. He'd made up his mind not to shoot unless I forced it.

I stood. He pointed to an open clothes closet.

I said, "You want me to go there?" It was a try at prodding him to say something, just to hear his voice. There were a couple other things I'd have liked to try even more. But with that mask I couldn't gauge the state of his nerves. He didn't want to make that loud noise with the gun, and I didn't want to push my luck. Standoff.

He didn't say a thing, just continued to point at the closet with his free hand and at me with the Python. I moved sideways to the closet, watching him. His gun and the dark holes behind the slits in his mask followed me. I stopped in front of the closet. He gestured again. I took a breath and backed into the closet. It was better than being out of it with a hole through my skull.

He pushed the door. It locked in place when it closed. There was no way to unlock it from inside; the only knob was on the outside of the door. Closet makers don't give much thought to somebody having a problem getting out of one.

It was dark and stuffy in there. And hot. I thought about him sweating under that ski mask. But he wouldn't be wearing it anymore. That was just something he carried with him for emergencies—like my walking in on him, or having to get away if there was danger of being spotted and recognized. Very professional. Prepared for everything.

I put my ear to the door and listened. There were small sounds. He was moving things around, shoving drawers back in place. I hoped that he'd started his search upstairs and was close to finishing the job down here.

What he was up to was obvious. He was the cleanup man, looking for any loose ends that needed to be removed. Judging by the fact that I hadn't spotted any signs of forced entry, he was probably the same one who'd gotten into Pilon's office and apartment, and into Crow's studio.

That didn't tell me if he was the only one involved, or the main one, or working for someone. Nor if he was just a cleanup man or a killer as well. What it also failed to tell me was *what* was being covered up.

I hoped he wasn't as good at spotting the things that needed removal as he was along other lines. If he was, there wouldn't be much left for me after he had gone.

It's hard to judge passage of time when you're locked in the dark. My body temperature was raising the heat inside the closet. I hadn't heard anything out there for what seemed a long while. Keeping my ear to the door, I began a silent count. When I got to five minutes I decided to break out.

Then I heard something and stopped myself. I listened

harder. The next sound was unmistakable: the apartment door being shut.

I waited another couple minutes. There were no further sounds.

The closet was shallow for what I had to do. But the width was just right. I braced my hands against the side walls at the height of my waist, pressed my shoulders against the back wall, and raised my feet off the floor. I brought my knees up to my chest and rammed both heels against the door just above the lock.

It crashed open on the first try. The force of my kick tumbled me to the floor, half out of the closet. I took a few deep breaths as I got up and then did a fast preliminary tour of both floors of the apartment.

He had put things neatly back in place the way he'd found them. The antique silver statue of a mermaid that Gilles kept on his desk was still there. Anne-Marie's fur coats were still in their storage closet. He hadn't been interested in the kind of valuables an ordinary thief would take. Neither was I. I went through the apartment again, carefully this time, to see if he had missed anything that would be of use to me.

One thing I knew he'd gotten: a good look at my face. Next time we ran into each other he would know me, faster than I would recognize him.

That could pose a hazard. I intended to meet him again.

Anne-Marie's appointment calendar wasn't in her work-room, or anywhere else in the apartment. Neither were any of her old check stubs or credit card statements. No letters, diary, stray notes, or anything else that would give me a lead to where she'd gone and whom she'd met over the past months.

Nobody was likely to notice these things were missing

for a long time, if ever. If someone did, innocent explanations were easy to come by. She could have taken the appointment calendar with her and left it somewhere. She could have thrown away the rest, as people do from time to time with old stuff.

I cursed softly and went back into Gilles's study. The cleanup man hadn't been interested in Gilles's appointments or financial statements. I went through his appointment book, back to the first of the year, without finding anything significant. Then I tackled his check stubs and credit card statements.

I found something in the latter that caught my interest, though I didn't know if it had any significance.

Six times that year Gilles had charged meals at a restaurant in Paris named Chez Solange. There were two successive dates in January, one date in March, and two more successive dates and one two days later in June. The amounts of the bills in each case indicated dinner for two.

I had spent time with Gilles in Paris. He liked to eat at either Balzar or Julien. It was easier for Gilles to relax in accustomed surroundings, where he knew the people and they knew him. Even with business meals he usually persuaded the people he was meeting to meet him at one of those two restaurants.

Checking back through his appointment book, I confirmed that the only times that year he'd been to Paris were around those dates: in January, March, and June. During each of those times Gilles had also dined at Balzar and Julien. But his having gone so often to a place other than his two favorites meant something. I didn't know what, and I didn't know if it was important. But at some point I'd checked out Chez Solange. So far I didn't have anything else.

I went up to the apartment library and got the most recent photo album down from the shelf. The latest pictures were all of Alain, but in some the boy was with his father or mother. I took one in which Anne-Marie's face showed clearly and another with a good close shot of Gilles next to his son.

There were easier ways I could have gotten recent pictures of them than breaking into the apartment. The photos were the *least* important part of what I'd come looking for. But that, and the fact that Gilles had dined with somebody six times in a Paris restaurant I'd never heard of, were the only things the cleanup man had left me.

Perhaps the pictures and that bit of information would prove to be of no use at all. I was used to that. Pointless follow-throughs were part of almost every case I worked on. So was stubborn persistance.

The cleanup man's job was to remove loose ends. Mine was the opposite side of the same coin. Keep plucking out any loose ends that were still left. Most of them would be short and meaningless. Wasted effort.

Then, if you got lucky, finally one of those ends wouldn't be loose. You'd find it knotted to the end of another and longer thread. You pulled that out, and it was attached to still another. And you kept pulling—until it was all out there in the open for you to look at.

ON MOST DAYS the Nice flower market fills the Cours Saleya with its heady melange of strong colors and fragrances. But on Mondays that long, broad esplanade at one edge of the Old Town is given over to the weekly flea market. I stood waiting between one stand displaying vintage postcards and stamp collections and another of old clocks and watches ranging from junk to antiques. The sky remained clear, but sporadic gusts of wind flapped the pink and blue awnings over the merchants' wares, warning of a change of weather on its way.

The hot gusts were forerunners of a sirocco, coming all the way across the Mediterranean from the Sahara, carrying fine particles of sand. In spite of my sunglasses I had to narrow my eyes against the blown grit.

That wasn't the only discomfort caused by the wind. I had to keep at least one button of my jacket buttoned, regardless of the heat. Any gust that blew my jacket open would expose the gun I was now carrying holstered under my left armpit. And if anyone spotted that, I'd be in serious trouble.

A private detective in France has no more right to carry a concealed weapon around in public than any private citizen. Doing so could lose me my license and get me kicked out of the country. But after my encounter with the cleanup man and *his* gun the risk of being caught with it by the police was less scary than the risk involved in running into him again. Or another like him. It had turned into that kind of job.

I'd gotten the gun out of its hiding place inside the rear seat of my car after leaving the apartment. The one I kept in the Peugeot was a compact semiautomatic—a Heckler & Koch P7 with eight 9mm rounds in its magazine. It lacked the punch of a .45 but was smaller, lighter, and extremely accurate. Also it fitted snugly in the shoulder holster without making a telltale bulge in my loose-fitted jacket. The sense of fallback security made up for the discomfort of carrying it.

A few minutes before two P.M. the door of the elevator from the parking garage under the Cours Saleya opened, and Nathalie stepped out.

She looked anxious but with her nerves under control. Nathalie's character had always been strong—capable of coping with situations that drove others to hysteria.

She was slender and elegant in a red and blue sailor blouse and straight blue linen skirt. A younger and taller edition of her mother. At thirty-six she even had the start of Mona's humor and concentration wrinkles, in the same places.

She put her arms around me, and I held her while she rested her head briefly against my shoulder. "Anything new," she asked, "since we talked on the phone?"

"Arlette is in the *juge d'instruction*'s office," I told her. "When she comes out she'll let us know."

"I don't know her," Nathalie said. "I've met the Bonnets a few times, but I don't know them that well, either." She looked up into my eyes. "It's *you* I'm counting on to get Crow out of this."

It reminded me of a summer long ago—Nathalie must have been ten—when we'd gone swimming and I'd taken her further out than I usually did. Gilles was on the beach searching among the rocks for shells and unusual sea pebbles. He was a good swimmer, but his skin reacted badly to the salt if he stayed in too long. On the way back Nathalie had called to me calmly, "I can't make it the rest of the way." She'd floated there, bobbing up and down in the heavy swells until I reached her, utterly confident I would get her safely to shore.

She linked her arm in mine as we strolled between the crowds around the flea market stands, going toward the end of the Cours Saleya that led to the opera house and the Palais de Justice. "I'll do my best," I told her.

An unexpectedly heavy gust of wind bounced a corner of a porcelain-and-glassware stand beside us. A tall vase tilted and fell off. I did a fast, low sideswipe and surprised myself by catching it one-handed, inches above the pavement tiles.

Nathalie said, "Your best is still pretty good."

The flea market vendor had tears in his eyes as he took the fragile vase from me. "It is my best piece. A genuine Gallé. Anything you or Madame wish to buy, I sell you at what I paid for it. Not a *sou* profit."

"We can't stop now," Nathalie told him. "But I may remind you of that one day."

"I won't forget you," he promised.

As we walked on I asked Nathalie, "Where did you spend last night outside Paris?"

"With a couple named Larre. Casimir and Paule Larre. You don't know them. They have a country house near Versailles." She cocked her head to peer at me. "You're checking on whether I have a solid alibi for last night, is that it?"

"The more I know, the better," I said. "I guess you went to Paris to think over your relationship with Crow."

"Yes. And decided I was being childish. I would have

come back today even if this hadn't happened. Crow is a crazy man, but I'm crazy, too. Crazy about him. If he has to work his way through some kind of premature midlife crisis, my place is here, helping him get through it.''

''Do you think he was having an affair with Anne-Marie?''

''No. Definitely not with her. Crow is too fond of Gilles for that.''

''Other women?''

''I don't know of any, but it's possible, certainly. That's one of the things I had to think out. But I do know he's in love with me. So any other woman would be temporary. Part of his crisis. Needing to reassure himself of his sexual prowess, in addition to proving to himself that he's still young enough to start a new career from scratch. I can survive both problems.''

We reached Rue Gassin and turned right, away from the opera house, going toward the Palais de Justice. ''Do you know any of the men Anne-Marie was seeing?''

''No. That's the one way in which she and Gilles were alike—not being very open with people.''

The Palais de Justice contains the law courts and the offices of a variety of legal functionaries, including those of the *juges d'instruction*. A wide, high flight of stone steps leads up to three entrance doors. Each door has one part of the three-word slogan of France over it: ''Liberté . . . Égalité . . . Fraternité.'' Everybody uses the middle one. I've never seen the Liberty and Fraternity doors opened. Nathalie and I sat down at a sidewalk table on the other side of the square, in front of the Café du Palais, to wait for Arlette. I ordered black coffee. Nathalie asked for a *bébé*—a very small whiskey on the rocks.

I told her, ''I don't know anybody Anne-Marie has been close to over the past few years. Male or female. Do you?''

"There's a woman who used to be a publicist in Paris when Anne-Marie was a model." Nathalie concentrated, trying to remember the name.

"Pascale Roca?"

"That's the one. You know her?"

"Anne-Marie introduced me to her once in Paris. But that was long ago. I didn't know they still saw each other."

"They got together again when Pascale moved down here about four years ago. She runs a beach place over on Cap Ferrat in the summer seasons. Calls it the Plage d'Or. I think she does publicity jobs in Cannes the rest of the year. She's the only one I can think of that Anne-Marie may have confided in—if that's what you're looking for."

I nodded. "That is what I'm looking for."

Nathalie had consumed her whiskey and I was finishing my coffee when Arlette emerged from the Equality door of the Palais de Justice. She came briskly down the steps with her briefcase tucked under one arm and threaded her way toward us between the triple line of cars parked in the middle of the square.

She was simmering when she took a seat at our table. "Xavier Escorel is *not* my favorite *juge d'instruction*. He won't let me see Frank Crowley, and he won't let me read the dossier he's so far assembled on this case."

"That's his right," I said.

"It's also his right to give me access to both client and dossier, if he chooses to. I know several other *juges* in there who would. It's our bad luck to be stuck with Escorel."

I introduced her to Nathalie. They shook hands politely and sized each other up quickly as belonging to the same small breed: those who are lucky enough to be sure of both their allure and their professional competence. Neither appeared envious of the other—merely normally wary, not sure at this stage whether they would become friends or just acquaintances.

"When can *I* get to see my husband?" Nathalie asked Arlette.

"The same time I can. By tomorrow morning Escorel has to either formally charge him as a suspect or let him go."

I said, "He won't let him go." They both looked at me, and I told them, "The bullets that killed Anne-Marie and Pilon *were* fired by Crow's gun."

"How did you find that out?" Arlette demanded. "I wasn't able to."

"I have a friend in ballistics. He owed me a favor."

"He took a big chance."

"No, all I told him on the phone was that it's been a long time since we've talked to each other. He went out to a public phone a few blocks away and called me back from there."

"Don't make it sound so easy," Arlette said. "Good work."

The barman came out and Arlette ordered a glass of Riesling.

"You ought to stick to local wines wherever you are," I told her. "The preservatives in wine that travels that far—"

She cut in with: "Don't teach your grandmother to suck eggs." Arlette picked things up quickly and was overeager to use them.

Nathalie shot me an annoyed look and asked Arlette, "Does this mean my husband is certain to be put in prison?"

"I'm afraid so," Arlette told her, "with a *juge* like Escorel. If your husband's gun killed them—"

"But *he* didn't kill them with it."

"That's right," I said. "So it'll only be provisional detention—until we break Escorel's hold on him. And we *will*."

The barman brought out Arlette's glass of wine. I paid for our drinks. After he went back inside she told Nathalie, "Until then you'll be able to visit your husband every day except Sundays and Thursdays. From nine until eleven-thirty in the mornings and from noon to 5 P.M. You should pack a bag to take to him. Changes of clothing, toilet kit, any sweets he likes."

"Make sure to include soap," I added. "French prisons don't supply inmates with soap."

Nathalie looked horrified. "But—that's barbarous."

I decided not to tell her that French prisons also only allowed one shower a week. The rest of the time Crow would have to make do with a small basin of water brought into his cell. I'd seen him get by with less. But the thought of it would bother Nathalie more than the actuality would Crow.

For a moment I thought she was going to cry. Then the moment was gone, and she nodded and said calmly: "I'll start getting things together for him as soon as I get home."

Arlette drank some wine and told her, "I'd like you to come to my office first so we can have a long talk. You may come up with *something* that will help me do my job. By the way, do you know when your brother is due back?"

"He's on a plane now. He'll arrive in the morning."

"After two flights that long, back to back, he'll have awful jetlag."

"Jet travel doesn't faze Gilles," I said. "It's jet society he can't stand."

Nathalie looked at me and nodded. That had been one

of the problems between him and Anne-Marie. Probably
the smallest one.

I asked Arlette, "Have you found out anything about
August Pilon so far?"

"He has an aunt in Paris," she told me. "She's the one
who raised him. According to an attorney who used Pilon
frequently, he always stayed with the aunt when he was up
there. The attorney doesn't have her name or address, but
Pilon gave him her phone number in case he had to get in
touch with Pilon in Paris."

She got the number from her briefcase, copied it on a
page from her notebook, and gave it to me. I put it in my
pocket and looked at Arlette with the respect she deserved.
"You do good work, too."

She smiled. "Thank you. It's nice we appreciate each
other. But it looks like we're going to have to postpone
this evening. I still have to work on the dossiers of those
other three cases for the Bonnets, and I won't be able to
get to them until late. A long night of work ahead."

Nathalie was looking thoughtfully from Arlette to me. I
ignored that and told Arlette, "There'll be other evenings."

"There had better be, or I'll sic that cobra on you."

As it turned out, I got to see her father sooner than I
expected.

🔯 **14** 🔯

SOCIETY PAGE COLUMNISTS unable to dream up enough scandal sometimes resort to enlightening their readers about the "most desirable" places to live on the Côte d'Azur. Some name two locations, others four or five. Whatever the number, the long, slender-necked peninsula of Cap Ferrat is invariably listed as one of them.

Cap Ferrat's small walled estates contain celebrated villas and gardens that switch owners with each sharp shift in the world's economy. Who is currently buying which villa from whom is a better indicator of changing fortunes than *The Wall Street Journal*. Cap Ferrat estates go where the money is.

Their inhabitants used to be people like Somerset Maugham and Jean Cocteau, Divid Niven and Rex Harrison, the Grand Marnier family and the Rothschilds. The new names tend to be oil-rich Texans and Arabs, with a sprinkling of major Italian tax dodgers.

With the high ridge in the middle of Cap Ferrat, every place there is on a slope with a view of sea and mountains. One side looks across the Bay of Villefranche to Nice and the Esterel Massif, the other across the Gulf of Saint Hospice toward Beaulieu and Monaco. The Plage d'Or was on the latter side, in a sheltered spot under a slope of umbrella pines and lofty eucalyptus trees. From the table where I was having my late lunch I could see the small cape behind which my own modest house and cove were hidden.

I hadn't eaten since breakfast, and lack of sufficient sleep the night before was catching up with me. My lunch centered around a large order of grilled *daurade*: a salt-water fish with plenty of protein and iodine to restore my energy and wake up my brain.

My table was one of a dozen on a raised deck that also held the kitchen and a curved bar with a roof of interwoven palm fronds shielding it from the sun. Below the deck the shingle beach had rows of orange mattresses and green shade umbrellas. Most of the men using them were middle-aged and paunchy; most of the women were younger, lissome, and topless.

There were twenty small changing cabanas and two shower stalls. A number of woven-rope walks crisscrossed the beach and a short pier jutted out over the water so that people could get from their mats and into the sea without crippling the soles of their feet on the sharp little stones.

Nobody was swimming that afternoon. The wind had grown steadier and stronger, churning up small whitecaps on the surface of the water. The five yachts that had come out of the Beaulieu marina and anchored off the beach were rolling a bit in the swells. It didn't seem to disturb the people sunbathing in the nude on their decks. But only two sailboards were out. The boy on one of them knew what he was doing, using the wind to skim along at high speed. The young guy on the other had spilled over into the sea at least seven times while I'd been eating and was in pretty much the same place as when he'd started.

I ate the last forkful of *daurade* and took a cool sip of dry white Bellet, a light local wine with a delicate aroma, while I looked around for Pascale Roca.

She'd been busy when I had gotten there, and I'd sent word I wanted to see her when she got free. She was still busy, I saw, helping her two beachboys carry trays of drinks to beach loungers too lazy to come all the way up to the bar.

The beachboys looked almost like twins. Sun-bronzed young athletes with the muscles you get from dedicated weight lifting. Each wore only a *cache-sexe*, a coy G-string affair with a pouch just sufficient to enclose their genitals. Pascale Roca wore loose dungarees, an oversized shirt with long sleeves, a peaked fishing cap, and rubber sandals.

In Paris, I remembered, American clients of hers had dubbed her "the Rock." She looked it: big and strong, almost my height, buxom and wide-shouldered. In the years since Paris I'd forgotten exactly how she looked. When I had sat down and spotted her on the beach it had suddenly made me think about the character in the ski mask and loose nylon jacket whose voice I hadn't been allowed to hear.

But her broad hands were long-fingered, and no jacket could have entirely concealed that bosom. Though the danger of running into the cleanup man was real, I warned myself not to get paranoid about it.

I was the last lunch customer in the platform's dining section. At the table next to mine a couple of bankers, one French and the other German, were finishing after-lunch drinks while arguing about whether to buy or sell dollars. Their utter lack of comprehension about what made any currency go up or down was enough to send the uninformed masses scurrying back to the barter system.

Getting up, they called to two women at the bar and headed back down to their beach mattresses. The women slid off barstools and strolled after them lazily. One was a voluptuous Scandinavian blonde. The other was darkly exotic: Ethiopian or Yemenite. Each had the top of her one-piece bathing suit rolled down to a neat thin strip well below the navel. The dark one's strip was white, the blonde's was purple. They went by me discussing what gowns they intended to wear to the Monte Carlo Red Cross Gala.

A dinghy with an outboard motor was on its way in from one of the yachts, carrying two young couples. Pascale Roca and her beachboys went over to meet it. They pulled the dinghy all the way up onto the beach and helped its passengers out. The two couples climbed the five steps and settled onto barstools. The beachboys went off to see if anybody else on the beach required service. Pascale Roca glanced up and down the beach, checking on whether anything else demanded immediate attention. Finally she came up onto the dining deck and scanned the eaters and drinkers.

Her broad face had always been plain but not unattractive. Now it was badly sunburned and dried out, almost ugly. I remembered that she'd never given a damn what she or anybody else looked like. Anne-Marie, back in those days, had begun to be edgy about being regarded as a pretty toy. It had been one basis for their friendship.

I raised a hand and signaled Pascale Roca. She came over and stood frowning at me.

"Remember me?" I asked her.

"Not your name. But I do remember you were one of Anne-Marie's boyfriends." No hostility there. No warmth, either.

I asked, "Have you heard what happened to Anne-Marie?"

"It was on the radio this morning. About her being murdered." Her frown got tighter. "I remember now—you're a detective. If that's what you came to see me about, it's wasted time. I don't know anything about it. And I don't want you to involve me."

"She was your friend."

"I *thought* she was. And then she dropped me like . . . That wasn't the act of a friend. Blaming me for everything."

"Everything," I repeated. "What are we talking about?"

"I told you," she said fiercely, "I don't want to get involved in it. Anne-Marie's dead, and that's too bad, but it's got nothing to do with me. I haven't seen her in a long time, and I don't know who killed her or why. And it's not a subject I have any interest in discussing. It's none of my business."

"That's enough!" I growled, startling her. "We both know you're not tough just because you look like you are. It's stupid to pretend you're something you're not."

She looked away from me, out to where the guy with the sailboard had overturned again, holding herself stiffly.

I said, "She *was* your friend. Your friendship hitting a bad patch doesn't change that. I have to find out what was going on in Anne-Marie's life that got her killed. You may be the only person in the world she trusted and cared for enough to tell about her personal problems."

She still wouldn't look at me.

I said, "Please sit down and let me buy you a drink."

She turned suddenly and called to the bar, "Bring me a brandy, Maurice." Then she sat down across the table from me. Her expression had lost its hardness. Her eyes had a wet shine. "Anne-Marie really hurt me," she said softly. "Turning on me like that. It wasn't *my* fault."

"What wasn't?"

She clenched her big hands together on the table, squinting down at them, brooding.

"Let's try it one step at a time," I said quietly. "Do you know about any of the men she had affairs with?"

"I know about the one who got her in trouble," she

blurted. "*Him*—not me. He . . ." She stopped herself from going on with it.

"Anne-Marie is dead now," I said. "Nothing you say can hurt her. The only thing you can do for her is help me find out who murdered her."

The barman brought a large brandy to our table, set it in front of her, and went away. Pascale Roca picked up the glass and took a long swallow. "The way her husband treated Anne-Marie," she said angrily, "it's no wonder she went to bed with other men."

"How did he treat her?"

"He decided she only married him because he was Mona Vaillant's son and business manager. He turned into an ice cube with her because of it. Hell, of course that was part of what made him attractive to her. Part of the package. Like Anne-Marie's being beautiful was part of *her* whole package. Would he have married her if she was dumpy and homely?"

She was right all the way. I'd known that was the major problem between Gilles and Anne-Marie. But there had been no way to make him understand it that way. Gilles had very few people he allowed himself to trust emotionally. He could never forgive any of them he thought had tricked him into that kind of trust. He was wrong, but that was Gilles.

"So she consoled herself with other men," I said. "That's not a crime. But one of them got her in trouble."

Pascale Roca rolled her glass between her rough palms, gazing down into the swirling liquor as though consulting it. "There weren't actually that many men she went to bed with . . . only a few. And never any one of them for long. She didn't really care for any of them. Except Gardier. That was different."

"What's his full name?"

"Christian Gardier."

It didn't mean anything to me. "How *much* did Anne-Marie care for him?"

"I think she was in love with him. Or she thought she was, from the way she talked about him to me. And it scared her. Because she thought her husband had met some woman *he* had fallen for. That he'd divorce Anne-Marie if he thought he could get their son. Apparently he loves the kid as much as she did."

I scowled at her. "What was she afraid of? In a divorce, French courts almost always give custody to the mother."

Pascale Roca nodded. "Unless the husband can prove she's not a fit mother. That being with her might be bad for the child."

"How could Gilles prove something like that?"

"If he could prove Anne-Marie associated with unsavory people, wouldn't that do it? She thought so."

"It would depend on *how* unsavory they were," I said. "And how deeply she was involved with them."

"Well, her love affair with Christian Gardier was serious," Pascale Roca told me. "And he's a professional criminal. Smuggling, armed robbery—maybe worse she didn't tell me about."

I experienced a tightening at the small of my back.

"What does this Christian Gardier look like?"

⊠ **15** ⊠

"I NEVER MET him," Pascale Roca told me. "And Anne-Marie never described him to me. Except that he's good-looking and strong. And tender." She smiled dryly. "A tender criminal."

"Is he big or short? Thin or strongly built?"

"I don't know."

I repressed a frustrated sigh. "Did she tell you how she happened to meet this Christian Gardier?"

"She knew him from when she was a kid. They grew up in the same village. La Brigue. They were childhood sweethearts. That was before she moved to Paris. And before he went to prison the first time—for smuggling."

La Brigue is very close to the French–Italian frontier. Smuggling across the rugged mountains there is part of the region's heritage, going a long way back. Some people there engage in occasional smuggling all their lives, as a sideline, and never get caught. Christian Gardier had been unlucky, or careless.

"They never saw each other again," Pascale Roca said, "until—oh, I guess it's a year and a half ago, now. He got out of another term in prison, this time for armed robbery in Marseilles, and paid a visit to La Brigue. He didn't have any family left alive there. But he went to see Anne-Marie's parents—to ask where he could find her. They wouldn't tell him. But he found out from other people in the village.

And the next day, when she came out of the Mona Vaillant offices in Nice alone, there he was. Waiting for her.''

She took another long swallow of her brandy. It didn't leave much in the glass.

"When she told me about it later," she resumed, "she said it really threw her, seeing him there after all those years. He hadn't changed much from the way she remembered him, according to her. And the way he *looked* at her—that threw her, too. They drove up into the hills and talked a lot about the old days together. He told her he kept thinking about her in prison. That in the end it was only thinking about her that kept him sane.''

I said, "That kind of passion would be hard to resist."

"Well, *she* certainly couldn't resist it. Anne-Marie told me all her old feelings for Gardier suddenly welled up in her—and coupled with her anger at her husband. They made love right there—up in the hills. In the grass. And she said it was as though they'd never been away from each other.''

"And after that?"

"He had something he had to do back in Marseilles that night. But they agreed to meet again a few days later.''

"Marseilles is a long trip," I said. "Three hours by train, nearly that by car. Where did they get together the next time?"

"That's what Anne-Marie came to ask *me* about," Pascale Roca told me. "She wanted someplace to be with him that would be pleasant and *safe*. Out of season I still do publicity work. Mostly for show business people that come into Cannes for business festivals and conventions. The kind of people who have affairs while they're here. Little trysts they wouldn't want anyone finding out about. So Anne-Marie figured I would know the best places for it.''

She finished off her brandy and added flatly, "She *didn't*

tell me about her long-lost love being a criminal. Not until much later. If I had known that, I would never have—"

She was interrupted by one of the beachboys coming up to our table with a problem."

"Pascale, some of the customers are complaining. The wind's starting to blow over their umbrellas."

"So *close* them and put them away," she snapped at him. "It'll be shady soon anyway." She nodded toward where the shadows of the trees were beginning to spread over one end of the beach.

He shrugged and hurried off to carry out her instructions. She glared after him. "Helpless customers and incompetent summer workers—I make a living off them, and I loathe them."

"It's the same in resort areas all over the world."

"I guess so." She picked up her glass, saw it was empty, and put it back down.

"Let me buy you another."

"No, I get headaches if I drink too much."

I said, "You were about to tell me what you recommended to Anne-Marie."

"The Hotel Dhalsten. Do you know it?"

I nodded. The Dhalsten was beyond the other end of Nice and just past the Côte d'Azur Airport, in Cagnes-sur-Mer. It had been one of the grand old hotels in bygone times. But it had deteriorated to a point where there was talk of tearing it down. Until a hotel chain had bought the place, about five years ago, and renovated it.

Its exterior had been restored to its former turn-of-the-century glamour, and the interior had been revamped for modern luxury. Since then the Dhalsten had become a four-star favorite. Being that close to the airport made it handy for traveling businessmen, entertainers, and diplomats. And it was perfect for meetings between people who'd just flown in and others due to fly out.

It also developed a reputation as a good place for a discreet nonbusiness rendezvous. Its staff was trained to pay no attention to any visitors a guest might have, day or night. With two side entrances through which elevators could be reached without going through the lobby, guests and visitors could slip in and out easily without being noticed.

"Not a bad choice," I acknowledged to Pascale Roca.

"*She* thought so, too," she said with a touch of bitterness. "She thanked me for it after she met Gardier there the first couple of times."

"And they went on using it."

Pascale Roca nodded. "The only thing that sometimes spoiled it for her, Anne-Marie said, was always being afraid that her husband would find out. And that she'd lose her son because of it. By the time she told me that she'd also told me about Gardier having a criminal record. But by then she was too hooked on him for anything I could say to make her stop seeing Gardier."

"Until something went wrong. What was it?"

"I don't really know. Anne-Marie just phoned me one evening sounding almost beserk. That must have been . . . oh, almost a year ago. I can remember her exact words, and that crazy fright in her voice. She asked me what kind of *friend* I was, to send her to 'that awful hotel.' She was very acid with me. Said she never wanted to see me or talk to me again."

"Why?"

"That's what I tried to ask her, but she banged down the phone on me. I kept trying to call her back, but she always hung up when she heard my voice. Finally I gave up trying." Pascale Roca shrugged angrily. "I guess somebody she knew saw her in the Dhalsten. Maybe with Christian Gardier. But that's not *my* fault, if they got that careless."

I didn't say anything to that. But there had to be more to it than what she'd just said. Somebody seeing Anne-Marie in the Hotel Dhalsten—even seeing her with Christian Gardier—would not be enough to make her that crazy-scared. It did not add up to hard evidence that she was having an affair with a professional criminal. And that, I had a very strong hunch, was what someone had gotten their hands on. Maybe along with something else even more incriminating.

I drove away from Cap Ferrat and up into the hills around the Loup Valley.

The fastest way of getting what I wanted next was by going to visit the cobra.

⊠ **16** ⊠

THE TWO BIG Dobermans leaped at me with bared fangs and nerve-shattering snarls. They crashed into the chain-link gate and dropped back on all fours, legs spread, regarding me patiently and making low sounds deep in their throats. It was the sort of sound a cat might make when eyeing a trapped mouse. But it wasn't mice the dogs had been trained to make a meal of.

The gate was part of an outer chain-link fence that surrounded Marcel Alfani's property. There was an inner fence of the same kind. Alfani called the area between the fences, patrolled by the guard dogs, his "moat." The dogs had been trained never to touch the inner fence. All night, and sometimes during the day, it carried a high-voltage current of electricity.

One of Alfani's bodyguards emerged from the rambling, ranch-style house inside the double fences. There was a long-barreled revolver holstered on his belt and a high-power rifle with a scope sight slung over one shoulder. Perfectly legal, as long as he didn't go off Alfani's property with the weapons. Protection of domicile.

He studied me through binoculars, confirming that I was who I'd said I was over the intercom beside the gate. Alfani's bodyguards knew me. He went back inside to deactivate the electronic locks on the gate.

I waited. It was only a thirty-minute drive from Nice, but I had the feeling of being much further inland. This

was a world of forests and stretches of emptiness, surrounded by high stone mountains. It was the kind of scenery Marcel Alfani was most comfortable with. He was no
sea lover. He'd been born in the mountainous heart of the
island of Corsica, and his first experience of the sea had
been when he took a ship from Corsica to Marseilles at the
age of fifteen. He'd gotten violently seasick and had never
forgotten it.

His property took up an entire hilltop several miles from
the nearest town, the fourteenth-century fortified village of
Tourette-sur-Loup. There were no other houses in sight of
Alfani's, and nothing at all above it. Below it the hill sloped
down on all sides toward the sheer-walled gorges of the
Loup—the River of the Wolf.

The bodyguard appeared again and blew a whistle. I
couldn't hear it, but the dogs did. They raced off around
the moat between the fences and vanished from sight. The
bodyguard came toward me, opened the inner gate, crossed
the moat, and opened the outer one. He let me get back in
my car and drive through without first searching me for
weapons. Alfani had proclaimed me a member of his family.

He didn't have much family left. His four brothers had
been killed in their teens, in early battles among the gangs
of Marseilles. His first wife had died long before, without
offspring. His much younger second wife, the mother of
Arlette, had died six years ago. Alfani's family now consisted of his daughter, two unmarried sisters who had never
left Corsica—and me. It was an honor I didn't enjoy,
though it was sometimes useful.

I left my car on the gravel parking area. The bodyguard
relocked the gates, blew his whistle, and strolled off on a
routine tour of the grounds. I walked through the house
and spotted Marcel Alfani in his swimming pool out back.

A second bodyguard stood on the pool patio, dividing his attention between his boss and the surrounding scenery. Like the other, he had a heavy-caliber revolver holstered on his belt. The weapon slung on his shoulder was a pump-action repeating shotgun. I guessed the third bodyguard was inside sleeping, so he could take over at night. The three bodyguards proved that Marcel Alfani was indeed in retirement. When active in the *milieu*—the underworld—he'd never had less than six around him at any time.

Alfani was treading water in the deep middle of his pool. He didn't look like a gangster. He had a short beard as white as his glossy hair. He wore black-rimmed glasses that gave his dark, dignified face a scholarly expression. Very nearsighted, he could wear his glasses even when swimming because he never put his face under water. It gave him claustrophobia.

He waved and smiled. "Come in. We'll have a conference."

The idea of holding "conferences" in the middle of a swimming pool had come to him years before. It guaranteed that nobody attending the meeting was carrying a concealed bug.

"I didn't bring a bathing suit."

"So? We're all men here."

That was true. His bodyguards doubled as cooks and housekeepers. Alfani didn't feel comfortable with women. Odd, for someone who'd started his career as a sixteen-year-old pimp. Or maybe not so odd.

When I took off my jacket and hung it on a patio chair Alfani immediately noted the gun under my arm. "You take chances."

"Necessary."

"Are you hunting or hunted?"

"Both."

"Ah, in that case . . ."

I placed the holstered gun on one of the patio tables and stripped off the rest of my clothes. Alfani regarded me with open interest as I approached the pool edge. "It always amazes me how big you became. When I first knew you you were smaller than my hand. Your mother once let me feel you moving inside her."

That story bored me. I'd heard him tell it about a hundred times. I dove in and surfaced beside him, treading water, careful not to splash any drops on his glasses.

"If you have come to see Arlette," he said in the stilted, formal way he had of speaking, "I'm afraid she is working late tonight. She phoned to tell me so I wouldn't worry. A good daughter."

"I know she's working late," I said. "I also know she's married, so—"

"A stupid marriage," Alfani interrupted. "To a stupid man. Not strong and smart enough for her."

"Aren't you proud—somebody with your background winding up with a member of the nobility as a son-in-law?"

Alfani chose not to notice my tone in mentioning his "background." "That is not the kind of nobility that impresses me," he said. "I am much more proud of having saved the life of a woman who has since been awarded both the *Croix de Guerre* and the *Légion d'Honneur*. Along with her son. *You* are the kind of man Arlette should be married to."

"I'm not strong and smart enough for her, either. I'm not going to be your new son-in-law, Alfani."

"It would be good for both of you. And would give me pleasure. I have known you since before you were born. I don't like her marrying strangers."

I always detested his possessiveness toward me. I don't

like gangsters. I didn't forgive this one for having forced me to wreck my government career to save him. He knew how I felt and ignored it.

I said, "It's you I came to see. I need a favor." I explained what I wanted to find out.

"You know I am no longer in the *milieu*, Pierre-Ange. Information does not come to me as it once did."

"But you have associates in Marseilles who can find out these things for you."

"Not associates, not anymore. Just some men who might make certain small inquiries for me, as a courtesy."

And because they were afraid that if he got mad he might decide to go back into business.

"Swim," Alfani told me. "Enjoy my pool. I will use the telephone. Be patient." He dog paddled to the side of the pool. The bodyguard was already there, waiting to help him climb out.

Alfani wasn't wearing a bathing suit either. Age hadn't robbed him of his look of physical strength. He was tall and heavyset without much fat. A peasant's build. Like the man in the ski mask. Too many people were built like that.

The bodyguard handed him a white terry cloth robe and draped a thick towel over his head. Alfani belted his robe and toweled the back of his head as he trudged into the house.

I began to swim. I prefer the sea, because that's pleasure, while swimming in a pool is just exercise. But I needed some exercise, and I probably wouldn't have enough strength left for anything but climbing into bed by the time I got home. I kept doing the length of the pool, back and forth, going at a good, steady clip. I got the exercise. It was more than half an hour before Alfani came out of the house.

He removed his robe and towel. The bodyguard helped

him climb back down into the water. He paddled over to meet me in the middle of the pool, and we had our conference.

"In answer to your first question," he said, "Christian Gardier is medium height and slim. Strong, but a lightweight—physically as well as in other ways."

One hunch gone awry. Gardier *wasn't* the cleanup man.

"He is still involved in a certain amount of theft and smuggling," Alfani told me, "but his main source of income since his last stretch in prison has been narcotics. He's a drug pusher. On a small scale. Everything Gardier does is small."

If someone could prove Anne-Marie was intimately involved with a drug pusher, *that* could have resulted in her losing her son.

"Gardier is an independent," Alfani continued. "Not a member of any *milieu* organization. Though, of course, he has to pay a percentage to one or he would not be allowed to operate."

"Which one?"

"Bernard Salamite's."

I'd heard about him. Among the Riviera mobs still fighting for pieces of Alfani's relinquished empire, Salamite was reported to be gaining control of the choice operations.

Alfani said, "Salamite doesn't know such a small-timer personally, naturally. After I spoke to him he had to make some phone calls of his own to check on Gardier. That's what took me so long."

"Did he find out where Gardier lives?"

"Christian Gardier doesn't have a permanent address. He changes residences frequently. Rooming houses when he is poor, hotels when he has money. But nobody in the *milieu* has seen him around in the past few weeks. Salamite is having further inquiries made, as a personal favor to me. I will phone you tonight if I learn more. Where will you be?"

"You can get me at home," I told him. "Find out anything about the Hotel Dhalsten?"

"No *milieu* organization controls it," Alfani said. "As a matter of fact, they have all been warned away from having anything to do with it. So whatever is going on there, nobody knows about it."

That was curious. "The warning would have to come from pretty high," I said, "to keep the mobs away from a choice plum like the Dhalsten."

"Very high," Alfani agreed. "From Paris. The government. Unfortunately, since I am no longer an active power I am not privy to exactly *who* in the government issued this warning."

High-level government protection for a Riviera hotel was peculiar. It *could* merely be because the Dhalsten was so often used by diplomats, French as well as foreign. Or it could be that something else was going on there that I didn't know about.

What I did know was that Anne-Marie and a small-time dope pusher, thief, and smuggler named Christian Gardier had used the Dhalsten for their rendezvous. And something had happened there that had terrified Anne-Marie. That she had been murdered months later might or might not be connected to what had scared her.

Either she or Gardier would have had to show identification when registering at the hotel. Neither would have wanted to use their real names. Gardier was the one who could easily obtain false identity papers. In his business he probably had several different identities ready for use when required.

I didn't know what name he had used at the hotel. But I had a good photo of Anne-Marie in my pocket, along with one of Gilles. They'd both been enlarged from the originals by a photo shop in Nice. I'd left the originals there before meeting Nathalie and picked up the results after leaving her and Arlette.

The Hotel Dhalsten was on my way home. I decided to drop in for a short preliminary check.

The wind from the Mediterranean hadn't penetrated the mountains around Alfani's house, and the sky was still relatively clear up there. But down near the sea the wind was in full force, pushing in a dense cloud cover and ground mist that was bringing on an early dusk. I turned on my low lights as I drove into Cagnes-sur-Mer and maneuvered through its narrow streets to the Hotel Dhalsten.

The first thing I saw when I got there was the guy I thought of as the cleanup man.

⊠ **17** ⊠

I COULD HAVE been wrong. All I saw was his back, for a few seconds.

I didn't think I was wrong.

The parking spot I'd found was a couple blocks away. I was approaching the Dhalsten's front entrance when I saw him. He was walking away from the hotel, and away from me. Wearing a dark gray business suit. He had a wide head and not much neck, and his hair looked dark in the mist. Tall and solidly built, long body and short legs.

As I'd been noticing all afternoon, a lot of men were built that way. What convinced me was the way he walked. A bit spread-legged, with his feet slightly turned out, balanced in a way that no man who spent most of his life behind a desk could manage. Sailors walked that way from always balancing on rolling decks. So did people used to sudden violence and ready to shift direction when it came. The man in the ski mask had moved that way when he had come to shut the closet door on me.

I followed him, quickening my pace to narrow the gap between us. The hard bulk of the H&K P7 holstered below my armpit was no longer annoying. If he was still carrying *his* gun, we'd be on more even terms this time.

He crossed the next intersection just before the traffic light changed. When I got there I had to wait until five impatient motorists gunned past before I could dodge across. By then my quarry was almost to the end of the next block. I went after him as fast as I could without running. He reached the corner and turned into the side street, and I lost sight of him.

When I entered the side street I couldn't spot him again. There were a lot of people hurrying to get to wherever they were going before the rain arrived. He wasn't one of them. I went through the side street to the next corner, but he was gone. He could have gone into any of a couple dozen buildings. Or jumped into a passing taxi. Or sprouted wings. I'd lost him.

I walked back to the main entrance of the Hotel Dhalsten. Maybe he hadn't come out of the hotel. He might have just happened to be walking past it. But I'd long ago learned to distrust coincidence.

The doorman was small and dressed in a scarlet and gold uniform with a white top hat that sported a large violet plume. He looked like he'd worn that outfit long enough to stop feeling silly in it. I held a fifty-franc note in my hand and described the man I'd just lost. The doorman eyed my money but shook his head. He didn't want to lose his job for lying to somebody who might be a police detective.

"If he just came out of here I didn't notice," he told me. "I've been busy helping people in and out of taxis."

I showed him the photograph of Anne-Marie and asked if he remembered her.

"I'm sorry, sir," he said, "but we're not supposed to talk to anybody about our hotel guests. Even ones who haven't stayed here in a long time."

That was good enough. If he remembered her, other employees would. I slipped him the fifty francs. He tucked it away and went to open the rear door of a limousine that had pulled up to the curb. I put the picture back in my pocket and went into the hotel.

The main lobby was marble and dark oak, stained glass and potted ferns. I asked the clerk behind the counter if he'd seen my man go out through the lobby: "My height, but heavier build. Short legs, the rest in his body. Dark gray business suit."

He frowned at me, trying to decide what I was. "I'm afraid that description is much too vague. So many people go in and out of here all the time. . . . As for a dark gray business suit . . ." He indicated himself. He was wearing one, too. He was also almost my height, and heavy. I saw his point.

He said, "May I ask—"

"Who's your chief of security here?" I cut in, hitting him with that tone of authority a cop doesn't forget once he's acquired it.

He blinked. "Monsieur Jacques Morel. Is there a problem? I can phone and see if he is in at the moment."

"Never mind," I told him. "I'll phone him myself later."

"If you would care to leave your name, I'll . . ."

But I was already walking away, back across the lobby.

Jacques Morel was not a name I knew. Most hotel security chiefs were former police detectives. I knew a lot of ex-cops, and I'd hoped the security man at the Dhalsten was one of them. Failing that, I'd have to find someone in the police that did have a good connection with this Jacques Morel.

It was Morel I wanted to show Anne-Marie's picture to next. He was the one who could help me find out what I wanted to know: about the times she'd been there with Christian Gardier—and what might have happened to scare her. But he wouldn't help unless he knew and trusted me, or I came guaranteed by somebody he did trust.

I went out of the hotel and around to one of its two side entrances. No doorman guarded this one, and the door wasn't locked. I went in, thinking how easy it would be for a thief to get in and out this way. But I hadn't heard of any robberies at the Dhalsten in the years since it had been renovated. That told me more about the potency of the hotel's high-level protection than what Alfani had said.

Inside, there was a marble hallway leading past a lounge bar to an automatic elevator. I stood there and scanned the hallway. It took a few moments to spot it: up in a corner near the ceiling above the elevator. The tiny eye of a closed-circuit video camera was registering my presence and probably putting it on tape. I'd seen others in the main lobby, but those had been more obvious. This one wasn't meant to be noticed.

Contrary to the Dhalsten's reputation, no guest or visitor entered or left without being seen and recorded.

I went into the lounge bar. It was a cozy room with a short bar and half a dozen curved, leather-padded booths. Four of the booths were occupied by well-dressed couples grumbling about the nasty change in the weather.

I sat at the bar, ordered a small cognac, and described the man I'd seen to the barman. Like the clerk in the lobby, he found the description too vague. I agreed with him, drank my cognac, paid for it, and went out. I had spotted three more carefully camouflaged video cameras in the cozy room. One aimed at the bar, the other two covering the booths.

It started me speculating on whether the booths were

bugged as well, to record any interesting conversations that occurred in them.

I was beginning to doubt that the Dhalsten's security man would give me much cooperation—unless I got a *very* good connection to him.

⊠ 18 ⊠

I DROVE FROM CAGNES-SUR-MER past the airport to Nice, ate dinner at a Tunisian restaurant in the Old Town, and then drove home. It was completely dark when I got there. I went through the house turning on lamps. I'd had two strenuous days without enough sleep between them, and I was worn out. My mind was a jumble of facts and hints and faces and questions. I intended to sink my brain into a solid ten hours of rest and recuperation before attempting to unscramble it all. But there were phone calls to make before I slept.

The answering machine had messages from Fritz Donhoff and Marcel Alfani, both asking me to call them back. First I phoned the Nice commissariat and asked for P.J. Inspector Soumagnac.

It took a while for them to locate him, and he came on the phone barking, "I'm busy. What do you want?"

I asked him if he knew the Dhalsten's security chief, Jacques Morel. He didn't, but he promised to ask around and see who did—when he found the time. Then he hung up on me and went back to work. I hadn't asked if there was anything new on Crow. He wouldn't talk about that over a phone in the commissariat.

I called Alfani.

"Christian Gardier has been in Naples," he told me, "attending to some business. He is returning to Marseilles aboard a cargo ship. It is due to arrive sometime after three tomorrow afternoon.''

"I want to be there to talk to him as soon as he comes off that ship.''

"I thought you might. There is a businessman in Marseilles—his name is Joseph Lepec. You should phone him when you arrive in Marseilles. He will introduce you to Gardier—and make sure Gardier answers your questions.''

He gave me Lepec's phone number. I copied it down, thanked him, hung up, and then called Fritz Donhoff.

"Your Anne-Marie *did* work for Serge Lotis before she became a magazine model," Fritz told me. "So she did know Lotis. Whether she saw him recently I don't know as yet. But I'm hoping to get something on Lotis's personal secretary, before long, that will open her up.''

"Anything else?" I asked him.

"Only confirmation of Madame Vaillant's suspicions. At least one of them. From an assistant designer Lotis fired a couple months ago. He told me Lotis suddenly changed all his designs for that couture collection of his, at the very last possible moment. Lotis claimed he'd gotten an inspiration. His former assistant doesn't know where the inspiration came from.''

I told Fritz about the aunt Pilon stayed with in Paris. But Fritz already knew about her. One of the women taking care of him would bring Pilon's aunt around to see him the following day.

Next I called Arlette's office. She was still there, with hours of work ahead of her. She'd had a formal notification from the office of *juge d'instruction* Escorel.

"He's going to put Crowley into provisional detention tomorrow. And keep him there while the case against him is further investigated. I'll meet with Crowley and Escorel in the morning. But I don't think I'll be able to make Escorel change his mind. He's making the point that Frank Crowley is an American, and that there's no way of guaranteeing he won't slip out of France and back to America unless he's kept in prison.''

I thought about the main prison of Nice—officially the *Maison d' Arrêt de Justice et Correction*. Its ugly, high-walled bulk covers a large chunk of an unlovely neighborhood of old factories and gimcrack apartments between the back of the Gendarmerie Nationale and a raised stretch of railroad freight tracks. As prisons go, it's not the worst. Crow could stand it for a while, but he wouldn't enjoy it. Prisoners have been known to be kept in provisional detention, without trial, for as long as a year and a half.

Arlette said, ''Escorel does have a strong case against Frank Crowley. Anne-Marie and Pilon were killed in his house and with his gun. He can't prove where he was when they were killed. Motive: he was romancing Anne-Marie, became furious when he came home unexpectedly and found her using *his* place to bed down with another man.'' She made a frustrated sound and added, ''So if you have *anything* I can use tomorrow morning against Escorel . . .''

''Not yet,'' I told her. ''You'll be the first to know when I do.''

When I hung up the phone I noticed my desk calendar was still on Sunday. I turned the page over to Monday—and saw what was written there: ''*Maidi.*''

It had been the beginning of the year when I'd marked her name in for this date, as a reminder. A good thing I had. In the press of the last couple days it had slipped my mind.

Opening my address book, I turned to her apartment phone number—in Bolivia.

The time difference made it still the middle of office hours there. But Maidi Phillips usually managed to wangle

her way out of working on her birthday. Being a civil serv-
ant has its advantages, if you know how to manipulate
intraoffice politics. Maidi knew how.

I dialed the overseas operator and gave him the number.
He told me there would be about an hour's wait. I gave
him my own number and promised I'd be there whenever
he could put the call through.

While I waited I took a shower and tormented myself
with bittersweet memories of Maidi. I put on a terry cloth
robe and espadrilles and walked out onto the brick-floored
patio behind the house, overlooking the sea. The wind was
still warm, but increasingly powerful. It was too dark to
see the cove below. I could hear the crashing of the surf
and the noise of thousands of pebbles being pushed and
dragged across the beach. You don't get surf like that in
the Mediterranean except during storms.

The storm hadn't broken yet, but it was coming. I looked
up and saw a few stars dart out from behind one dark mass
of cloud and swiftly vanish into another. I remembered a
night very much like this one when Maidi and I had spread
a beach mat on the patio and made love with the storm
building around us.

I remembered a lot of other things about the months
we'd been together. With Maidi, it had been the nearest
I'd come to wanting to get married again. Our feelings for
each other had been ripe for it. But the conditions weren't.

We had refused to give hardheaded thought to those conditions until the crunch came. Maidi was a State Department foreign service officer. She'd been serving at the
consulate in Nice when we'd met and fallen for each other.
The crunch had taken the form of a directive transferring
her to the embassy in Bolivia. That was when we'd finally
had to face the realities. For Maidi the transfer was a pro-

motion in rank, and she wasn't going to throw her career away in order to stay here with me. I wasn't prepared to spend my life trailing her around the world.

It was almost four months since she had gone.

The first big drops of rain were hitting my face when the phone rang. I went inside and picked it up.

But it wasn't the international operator. It was Fritz Donhoff again. His voice was more solemn than normal.

"Serge Lotis is dead."

I said, *"Merde . . ."*

"You have an indelicate way with the French language," Fritz said. "But in this case, yes, *merde* indeed. Lotis fell from the roof of his apartment building. Nineteen floors down to the sidewalk."

I said: *"Fell."*

"Or jumped. Or was pushed. The police are inclined to believe it was suicide. It is the simplest explanation for his going up onto the roof. And they have nothing at all to indicate he was pushed."

"When did it happen?"

"Almost two hours ago. I just learned."

"They're cleaning up," I said.

"They?"

I told him about my encounter with the cleanup man in the apartment of Gilles and Anne-Marie. If he was the same man I'd glimpsed outside the Dhalsten Hotel, he couldn't have been in Paris to throw Serge Lotis off that roof. There was more than one man at work on this cover-up.

"The question is," Fritz said, "*what* are they covering? It must be more than the theft of some fashion designs to warrant efforts on this scale. Including three killings."

I agreed with him. And I didn't have any more answer to the question than he did at that moment.

"There *is* one positive aspect of the death of Serge Lotis," Fritz said. "His misfortune will make my work easier." ·

"There's that," I said. People he would have had difficulty in pressuring into revealing secrets about Lotis would no longer have reason to protect him.

I put down the phone and stared at the wall behind my desk, pondering the big question.

The wall didn't tell me anything except that it could use a new coat of paint.

The phone rang again.

This time it was the international operator, ready to put through my call to Bolivia.

It wasn't Maidi who answered. It was a man, distinctly American: "Hello, Norris? I've been waiting for your—"

"My name is Sawyer," I cut in. "I'm calling long-distance for Maidi Phillips. Is she around?"

"Oh, sorry, I thought . . . Hang on a minute, I'll get her."

There was no logical reason to be startled at finding a man in her apartment. Maidi and I hadn't pledged fidelity to each other. That would have been ridiculous. It could be years before she got transferred out of South America. And then it could as likely be to the Far East as back to Europe.

Maidi came on the phone sounding just a bit awkward about it. "Peter? That was Bill . . . a friend from the embassy. He just dropped by and was expecting a—"

"Never mind," I said. "Happy birthday, Maidi."

"You actually remembered! Thank you."

"I don't forget anything about you," I told her.

"It's so good to hear your voice, even over this lousy connection. I miss you, Peter."

"The missing is mutual. Any chance of the embassy there getting tired of having you around soon?"

"No, damn it. And I hate it here. I just can't work up any real rapport with the Latin American mentality. My fault, I suppose. I don't feel at home here. I got too used to Washington and Europe."

There was a short silence between us. Then she said, "There *is* a possibility I might be able to wangle one week's holiday in Europe—at the end of this year or the beginning of the next. Is . . . would I be able to stay at your place?"

She meant had I installed somebody else in the house since she'd left.

"You're always welcome here," I told her. I didn't say what I thought: that spending that short a time together would make us both much too tense to enjoy it.

"I may really take you up on that," Maidi said. "My God, it would be a relief to be back in the *real* world— even for just a week. Things are so unpleasant here."

I didn't see any point in telling her that things weren't too pleasant at the moment back in the real world, either.

I turned off all the lamps and got into bed, listened to the rain slashing at the windows, and let myself drop into that solid ten hours' sleep.

19

I HATE EATING at home alone. Even breakfast. I had mine next morning in Edmonds, one of the three cafés in Cap D'Ail a few minutes from my house.

All three were packed that morning. Tourists glaring at the downpour outside and complaining about how much each ruined day of vacation was costing them.

What constitutes bad weather depends on your point of view. Riviera merchants love the rain. It drives people off the beaches and into shops and bars to spend their money. It also puts out forest fires and makes everything grow faster and greener.

After breakfast I drove west on the Lower Corniche to Nice and along the Promenade des Anglais to the Côte d'Azur Airport. I was dressed for the weather: light corduroy cap, full-length waterproofed Levi jacket, jeans tucked into short leather boots with ribbed rubber soles. I had a small overnight bag with me, in case I couldn't get back from Marseilles that evening. I also had my Heckler & Koch P7. Until this job was over I wouldn't be going anywhere without a gun, if I could help it.

The driving was hairy. New waterfalls cascaded down the cliffs onto the road. Every passing car threw a shower of dirty water against the windshield. Now and then a car would skid across the center line into the wrong lane. It was the first rain in three weeks, and a lot of oil that had soaked into the tarmac was rising to the surface. Too many

drivers were ignorant of that danger; they get delusions of
being Grand Prix drivers when they get near Monte Carlo.

I left my Peugeot in the airport's underground parking
and took the elevator up to the enclosed top-deck lounge.
Ordering a cappuccino and slice of *tarte aux pommes*, I
took a table by the glass wall overlooking the runways.
Waves were crashing across the ends of the newer runways
that had been built out over the sea. All outgoing flights
had been canceled. Including the short hops to Marseilles.
I'd phoned and found that out before breakfast. My trip to
Marseilles would be by train. In this weather it would be
too long and unpleasant a drive.

The control tower had its hands full directing arriving
planes. Gilles's Air-Inter connecting flight from Paris was
delayed forty minutes. I relaxed and waited. A Pan Am
747 from New York emerged from the fog, coming down
too steeply. It leveled off at the last moment, landed halfway down the longest runway, and just managed to brake
to a halt before it would have gone off the end into the sea.

The Air-Inter from Paris arrived twenty minutes later
and made a perfect landing. I waited until the buses were
bringing its passengers to the terminal and then went downstairs to meet Gilles at the baggage claim section.

"I imagine you think I'm a cold-hearted bastard," he
said. "Because I'm not standing here crying. I *am* sorry
about Anne-Marie dying like that. But . . ."

He didn't finish it. We were standing apart from the
crowd waiting around the long luggage belt. The belt was
moving now, but none of the bags from his flight were
coming out on it yet. Gilles didn't look like someone who
had just completed two days of flying halfway around the
world and back. He had special stores of inner strength.
Along with that knack essential for international business-

men: an ability to sleep through a flight and arrive prepared to meet people fresh and clearheaded.

He wasn't going to continue what he'd started to say, so I did it for him: "But the two of you haven't been happy with each other for a long time."

"She didn't love me," Gilles said stiffly. "She *pretended* to, in the beginning. Because she wanted to become part of the company. I admit she proved herself of value once she was in it. Mama came to have a great deal of respect for her. But after she became sure of that, Anne-Marie apparently found it increasingly difficult to keep up her pretense with me."

I said, "I had the feeling you two would have gotten a divorce if it weren't for your son."

Gilles grimaced and looked away from me. "Probably."

"Do you think she had lovers?"

He repeated the word: "Probably."

"Ever hired a detective to follow her and get proof?"

Gilles looked puzzled. "What would have been the point of that? I could have proved she had dozens of lovers and she would still have obtained custody of Alain if we divorced."

I said, "But now it's you who'll get Alain."

"Yes." He hesitated, torn between guilt and a stubborn honesty about what he felt. "I admit that was one of the first things I thought of after I heard what happened. I guess that was horrible of me."

My own feelings about that were mixed. It wasn't something I liked hearing him say. At the same time I realized it was a natural reaction for him to have, considering how strained the relationship had become between Gilles and Anne-Marie. Natural, but better left unexpressed. I sidestepped the implied question in his tone by asking one of my own:

"Do you think Crow could have been one of her lovers?"

Gilles thought about it and then shook his head. "No. Crow wouldn't do that to me. Besides," he added sourly, "Anne-Marie preferred men who were good-looking. Crow is an interesting man, but nobody would call him handsome."

"What about you?" I asked Gilles. "Do you have lovers?"

He tensed and didn't answer.

I took a shot: "In Paris, for example. The one you have dinner with at Chez Solange."

Gilles turned on me with an astonished, accusing stare. "You've been prying into my personal life."

I put a hand on his shoulder. He stayed tense, but I kept it there. "Do you think Crow killed Anne-Marie?"

There was no hesitation this time. "Of course not!"

"He's in prison for it. He's going to spend most of the rest of his life there unless I can prove he didn't do it. I need everything I can find out about Anne-Marie and every person associated with her. It's the only way I can eliminate innocent things and get to why Anne-Marie was murdered."

I felt his body relax a little under my hand. "There's no longer any reason to hide it," he said softly. "Her name is Jacqueline Crozet. She owns an antique shop in Paris. I met her at a business dinner. She was with another man, but we got to talking, and . . ." Gilles blushed suddenly. "She cares for me. I don't know why, but it's no pretense. She really does."

I hoped he was right this time.

"We usually dine at Chez Solange because it's near her apartment and there is no danger of running into anyone I know there."

"You were scared Anne-Marie would find out and use your affair to get a divorce. And you'd lose your son."

"Yes. It was hard for Jacqueline and me, always having to be so careful—so furtive."

I dropped my hand from his shoulder. "Now you don't have that problem."

"You suspect *me* of Anne-Marie's . . ." He couldn't say the word murder.

"No, I don't." I would still show his picture to people at Chez Solange and check on this Jacqueline Crozet, if I didn't come up with something more likely. But I didn't think the answer to the murders was with Gilles. "I need some help," I told him. "I want you to check on Anne-Marie's bank balance for me. How much is in it, what she's been spending. And I want to know what's in her safe deposit box."

"Her jewels are there," Gilles said. "She had a lot even before I began giving her jewelry. And her stocks and bonds. Anne-Marie began buying securities as soon as she was earning sufficient money. She was very thrifty, you know. Her parents had very little money. She was always afraid of winding up poor."

"I want to know if it's all still there."

"Why wouldn't it be?"

"Just find out. And get me copies of her credit card statements and the bank's photostats of checks she's used—over the last twelve months."

Gilles shrugged. "Okay. The funeral is tomorrow. After that I can decently look into—"

"I want to know sooner than that. By this evening."

"If it's that important . . ."

"I think so."

"I'll look into it today, then," he said, and he pointed to the luggage belt. "Here come the bags."

"I'll be in touch this evening," I said, and I went out to take a cab to the train station.

Aboard the train I took out my notebook. I wrote three names on one page: Anne-Marie Vaillant, August Pillon, and Serge Lotis. On the page across from it I wrote: "Christian Gardier . . . cleanup man . . . Hotel Dhalsten."

I spent most of the three hours to Marseilles putting together what I had so far that connected them with one another.

When I got off the train at the Gare Saint Charles I made the phone call from one of the public phones in the station lobby. I gave my name and asked for the man Alfani had told me about: Joseph Lepec. He came on the phone with a voice that sounded like his throat had been severely mangled in the past, and he was profusely apologetic.

"I'm very sorry to tell you that the *Stella Fortia*, the cargo ship Christian Gardier will arrive on, has been delayed by the storm. It is now expected here either tonight or sometime tomorrow. Can you call me again at eight this evening? By then I'll know which and can arrange to meet you and take you to meet him. I hope this does not inconvenience you."

It did, but I told him it didn't. His regret sounded entirely sincere. Lepec might not know I came from Alfani, but he'd been told to be nice to me by someone who scared him. Probably Bernard Salamite himself, currently the biggest man in the Marseilles *milieu*.

It was a few minutes past two in the afternoon. I decided to check into a hotel. If Christian Gardier got in early enough that night, I could check out and return home. More likely I'd be spending the night in Marseilles.

I got a cab outside the station and had it take me to the

Canebière, the bustling main street known to generations of English-speaking seamen as the Can-of-Beer. Most of the hotels are around there, along with the greatest concentration of bars, shops, and restaurants. I checked into the Hotel Provence, on the Cours Belsunce just off the Canebière. Then I walked a few short blocks to the Vieux Port, had lunch at the Cintra Bar on the Quai des Belges, and went for a long stroll around the port.

I didn't see anything there that bore any relation to the nearby Côte d'Azur. Marseilles is an ugly, grimy, lusty commercial harbor, the biggest anywhere around the Mediterranean. Everything about it is based on those thousands of cargo ships and tankers using its miles of docks. It's a merchant sailors' town and has been for a couple thousand years.

I was soaked from the rain when I got back to the hotel. After a drink at the bar I took a bath and shower and changed into dry clothes. By then it was after seven. Time to make a couple of calls.

My first was to Fritz Donhoff. August Pilon's aunt hadn't been able to tell him anything at all about what her nephew did in Paris. But the secretary of the late Serge Lotis had been more helpful. A man named August Pilon had phoned the office on Wednesday of the previous week and had asked to talk to Lotis. When she asked him to state his business, he'd said to tell Lotis there was going to be trouble over his last couture collection. Lotis had taken the call, gone out of the building a few minutes later, and returned in less than an hour extremely upset about something. He had made a call to Nice immediately after returning.

She also remembered that Anne-Marie had phoned Lotis about four or five months ago, and that he'd gone off somewhere to meet her. She had no idea what their meeting was about. Nor did she remember the exact date—but she'd promised Fritz to look it up in her office calendar as soon as she could. Along with checking the number in Nice that Lotis had phoned last Wednesday. The Lotis offices were closed for a couple of days because of his death.

My next call was to Gilles. He came on the line sounding puzzled and worried.

"It's going to take a couple of days to get photostats of Anne-Marie's checks and credit statements," he said, "but the rest of what you wanted . . . Pete, something has been going on that I can't explain. All of her jewelry is missing. I don't know where it is or when she removed it from the box, but . . . ."

"What about her securities?" I asked him.

"They're gone, too! I checked and found she had sold them all."

"When?"

"Over a period of a few months, beginning nine months ago. I don't know what she did with the money she got for them. It's not in her savings account. *That's* almost depleted. She used to have a considerable amount in savings, but she withdrew most of it. In cash."

"When?"

"Half of it almost a year ago. The rest the following month. It's not like Anne-Marie to strip herself financially like that. You know she wasn't a spendthrift or . . . I just don't understand it."

I didn't either, but I wasn't as surprised as he was.

At eight I phoned Joseph Lepec. He was sorry, but the ship carrying Christian Gardier wouldn't come in until shortly before noon the following day. Lepec gave me a place to meet him the next morning at eleven.

I had dinner in the hotel dining room and went back up

to my room to phone the Nice commissariat. I asked for Soumagnac. They told me he and his partner, Ricard, were out on an assignment and not expected back until the following evening.

I hung up, turned on the room's television set, and settled down to finish my day watching an old western. It was one of the good oldies—*My Darling Clementine*, dubbed in French.

I'd seen it before, but it still took some getting used to, hearing Wyatt Earp say: *"Arrête ta saloperie et haut les mains."*

It ended the way I remembered. Doc Holliday died nobly at the O.K. Corral. The Clanton gang got shot to pieces. Henry Fonda earned the love of Cathy Downes. I went to bed and got another full night's sleep.

🔲 **20** 🔲

THE RAIN HAD stopped, but there was fog so thick that everything half a block away was diffused into unreality. Garbage odors mixed with normal harbor smells of spilled fuel, dead fish, and stagnant water. It was shortly after one the next afternoon. I was climbing the hill of the Panier quarter behind the Joliette Bassin of the Marseilles docks.

The Panier always makes me think of the Dickens descriptions of criminal enclaves in Fagin's London. The fog made it more sinister than usual.

It's the birthplace of the Riviera *milieu*—a densely crowded warren of moldering dwellings where immigrants from all parts of the Mediterranean fight one another for living space and racket control. For over a century sailors have been warned against going in there. The worst danger is getting killed for your money and dropped down a deep hole to the rats in the sewer system. But dim bars and cheap whores continue to lure seamen there, and each year the same percentage vanish without a trace.

Not the smartest neighborhood for a stranger to explore without an eight-shot confidence booster.

I went up the steps of an alley where high walls leaned toward each other, almost meeting overhead. On a bright day little light would filter into the sloped alley. With the fog it was murky.

At the top was a bar called Les 4 Aces. I put my back to the wall across from it and waited.

Shadowy figures lurking inside deep doorways watched me but did not beckon or approach. I had arrived and planted myself there too purposefully to be a wandering fun-seeker. They smelled cop. A discriminating sense of smell is often important for survival in the Panier.

The bar had a wide, cracked window and torn lace curtains. Inside a pair of dim lamps revealed women on barstools waiting for the afternoon influx of customers while their men sat at tables playing cards.

This was where Joseph Lepec had told me to wait for Christian Gardier. I'd been right about Lepec's throat. There was an ugly knife scar across it, and another between his nostrils and upper lip. He was a minor functionary in Bernard Salamite's organization, responsible for some of the contraband that came and went by ship.

He had told me Christian Gardier's closest friend, the third engineer on the *Stella Fortia*, had helped Gardier sign on for this trip with forged oiler's papers. Gardier was supposed to get a package of uncut heroin in Naples and bring it to Marseilles. Seamen coming off cargo ships are seldom searched. Partly because cops in the dock areas are bribed, but mostly because of sheer impossibility. There are too many sailors leaving and boarding ships every day for all of them to be checked.

A man strode toward me out of the fog: stocky, wearing the dark cap of a merchant marine officer without insignia. He stopped when he reached me and said softly, "Joseph's man?" His face was badly pockmarked. His nose had been smashed long ago and never fixed.

I nodded and said what he was waiting for: "Sawyer."

He took my elbow and steered me away with him, not looking left or right. We went down the steps of another steep alley and turned into a blank-walled passageway. It ended at the roofless ruin of an old hospital. The building had been dynamited by an SS demolition team in the war because the hospital was suspected of hiding fugitive Jewish families and other anti-Nazi criminals.

We went through a hole in the wall and crunched across the rubble of shattered bricks, plaster, and tiles until we were between two fallen, fire-scorched roof beams. He let go of my elbow and made a short tour behind the remnants of inner walls around us. When he was sure nobody else was there he came back to me.

"Lepec says I should tell you anything you want to know. So ask."

"You're not Christian Gardier."

"I'm a friend of his from the *Stella Fortia*. Second engineer. My name's Jean-Luc."

"His best friend, according to Lepec."

"I guess so. Christian and me did time together in Les Baumettes. Three years in the same cell. I'm the one who got him into dealing drugs when he came out and moved in with me awhile. Better dough than what he did before." Jean-Luc wore a disgusted expression. "And safer, for anybody with the brains to be careful."

Les Baumettes is the maximum security prison outside Marseilles. I asked, "Where's Gardier?"

"In jail. In Naples."

If I flew down to Naples and pulled the right strings, I just might be allowed to see Gardier there. But not under conditions where he would talk freely. I asked Jean-Luc, "What happened?"

"Cops caught him with that bundle of heroin on him. Day we were supposed to sail." Jean-Luc shrugged. "His old problem. Christian was always too reckless, took too many chances. Got worse that way after his girlfriend dropped him."

"Which girlfriend?"

"Someone he used to go see in Nice. Anne-Marie something. I don't know her last name or I'd tell you. Lepec said not to hold back with you. But Christian never mentioned any last name."

"Tell me what Gardier did say about her."

"She was his girlfriend way back. They were from the same town. He talked a lot about her in Les Baumettes. At first just to pass time. Just remembering anything nice to cheer himself up, the way you do in prison. But by the time he finished the stretch he'd convinced himself he was still crazy about her."

Jean-Luc got out a small cigar and lit it. I recognized the acrid smell of the smoke that hung in the fog between us. Toscanelli—a cheap cigar imported from Italy. Even cheaper when smuggled in, avoiding customs duties.

"After Christian got out and I helped him start making money again," he told me, "he went off to look for this Anne-Marie. Found her in Nice. And the old fire was still there, according to him. He started going off to spend time with her whenever he could get away."

"Do you know where they got together?"

"Some hotel around Nice is all I know. He never mentioned the name. Just that he'd register under a fake name and she'd come join him in the room. They'd have food and drinks sent up, and—big romance."

Jean-Luc took a drag on his cigar and found it had gone out. That's one of the troubles with Toscanellis. He relit it and blew smoke my way. "Only trouble was, she was always nervous about it. Seems she was married now and had a kid. She was scared if anybody found out she was involved with Christian—a guy with his record—her husband would divorce her and be able to take the kid away from her."

His Toscanelli had gone out again. He cursed and flicked

it away. It bounced off a broken wall and fell into the rubble. He said, "Christian told me she started getting almost hysterical about that, too worked up to make love right. So finally he began calming her down by teaching her to snort a little coke with him first."

"In the hotel room," I said.

"I guess so. Where else? That's where they screwed after they snorted. Right?"

I said, "Tell me why she dropped him."

"Christian called her one day to arrange to meet her in Nice, like usual. She told him no. Told him to please stay away from her. Never come see her anymore. Well, he went to Nice anyway. Naturally. Picked her up somewhere out on the street and asked her what the hell was the matter. She almost screamed at him. She told him somebody had found out about them."

"Who?"

"Christian doesn't know. She wouldn't tell him—didn't want to talk to him at all. She just *begged* him to leave her alone. Never come see her again. She swore if he did—and she lost her kid because of him—she'd kill herself."

"When was this?"

"Oh . . . about a year ago, I guess. Thing is, Christian believed what she said—that she'd kill herself. So he never saw her again. And after that's when he started getting more careless than before."

I went back to the hotel. I'd checked out but had left my overnight bag at the desk. Using the phone booth behind the lobby, I called Marignane Airport outside Marseilles. Flights between there and Nice were still grounded, because of the fog now. My railroad schedule said the next train to Nice wasn't until six that evening. I put through a phone call to Laurent Soumagnac's apartment in Cap D'Ail.

His wife, Domiti, told me he was still sleeping.

"When do you expect him to get up?"

"I'm supposed to wake him before five. We've got a babysitter coming so we can go out for dinner before he goes to work tonight."

"I'll call again at five," I said, and I went for another walk.

When I phoned at five Soumagnac answered. He was more relaxed than the last time we'd talked on the phone.

"Sure I checked on the Dhalsten. I told you I would as soon as I got some free time. That's some hotel, you know. We're not supposed to poke our noses into anything that goes on there. Heavy government protection. I guess because so many government people use it. Ours and foreigners. Paris doesn't want them bothered—and the mayor's office in Nice passes the same instructions to their local police."

The Dhalsten was getting curiouser and curiouser.

Government pressure strong enough to keep out both the cops and the crooks.

From both national and local authorities.

"Did you find anybody with a contact to its head of security?" I asked Soumagnac.

"Jacques Morel—yes, but it wasn't easy. He's not local, and he doesn't fratronize with any of our men. Cagey, secretive character. His main police contact is with the Gendarmerie Nationale. Captain Rinaldi. He doesn't know much about this Morel either. Except that he came down from Paris to run security for the Dhalsten right after it was renovated. And Rinaldi has orders to cooperate with him—whatever Morel wants."

"Orders from where?"

"They came down the chain of command. You know

how that is. By the time something like that reaches us there's no way of knowing where it originated."

I said, "And that's *all* Rinaldi knows about Morel."

"Just about. Funny thing. When I told Rinaldi it was you asking about Morel he said Morel had just been to see him about *you*."

'That *is* funny," I said.

"But Morel didn't ask for you by name, which is funnier. He showed Rinaldi a couple pictures of you and asked if he knew who you were."

Captain Rinaldi did know me. And I knew him. I phoned him at the Gendarmerie Nationale.

"When this Jacques Morel asked you who I was," I said, "did he tell you why he wanted to know?"

"No," Rinaldi told me. "And I didn't ask. Those are my orders. Cooperate. Answer anything Morel puts to me, don't ask him anything."

"What kind of pictures of me did Morel show you?"

"Ordinary photographs. A little fuzzy, but I didn't have any trouble recognizing you."

"Do you remember what was around me in either of them?" I asked Rinaldi. "Any special background?"

He thought for a bit. "Couldn't see anything in one of them. In the other, you're at a bar. Looking straight up at the camera."

"Up," I repeated.

"That's right. As though the photographer was shooting down at you from the top of a ladder or something. You're looking up at the camera, and you've got a drink in your hand. Looked like a brandy glass."

My spine was already too tight. It got tighter.

I said, "Tell me what Jacques Morel looks like."

Rinaldi told me.

It didn't come as a complete surprise by then. I remembered giving part of that description to the clerk and barman in the Hotel Dhalsten.

My last call before going to catch my train was to Arlette's office.

As soon as she heard my voice she began talking and didn't give me a chance to say anything for a while.

"I talked to Frank Crowley's partner, Gilbert Promice. He has nothing to gain out of Crowley being in prison. He has to continue paying him the same amount every year for ten years, no matter what. And he *needs* Crowley. There are areas of the business he doesn't know so well. Part of their agreement is that Crowley will continue to act as a consultant. Promice even gave me a list of important questions to ask Crowley next time I visit him in prison. I'm positive he didn't have anything to do with framing him."

"So am I," I told her. "I want you to book me a hotel room in Nice for tonight. The Napoleon would be good. It's near your office, and nobody there knows me. Go sign in and say your husband will be using it. So I don't have to show my own papers when I get there."

"What's going on?" Arlette asked me.

"About now some people may be deciding it would be a good idea to kill me," I said. "So far their killing record is impressive. I don't want to go home tonight and give them a chance to improve that record."

🔲 **21** 🔲

"LET ME SEE if I have your thinking straight," Arlette said. "You believe every room in the Dhalsten probably has bugs and hidden video cameras. Which recorded Anne-Marie going to bed with her drug-pusher boyfriend over a longish period—as well as using illegal narcotics with him."

She had picked me up at the Nice railroad station and was driving me to the airport to get my car. It was raining again, but lightly. The wind had changed. Now it was a Mistral, blowing down the Rhone Valley and swinging east along the coast, scattering clouds. It would probably be clear by morning.

"You further think," she said, "that this planting of listening devices and video was done when the Hotel Dhalsten was renovated—by an intelligence service of the government. Which service are you talking about? DST? DGSE?"

The Interior Ministry's DST—*Direction de la Surveillance du Territoire*—bears some resemblance to the FBI, but it is supposed to concentrate entirely on counterintelligence within the boundaries of France. The Defense Ministry's DGSE—*Direction Générale de la Sécurité Extérieure*—is much like the CIA, conducting espionage and counterespionage operations abroad. In theory, they're not allowed to encroach on each other's territories. In fact, they often do.

"It *could* be one of the other intelligence outfits," I said. "The Police Nationale's RG branch, for example. Or the Gendarmerie Nationale's *Groupement d'Intervention*. France has quite a few. But the DST and the DGSE are the biggest, so they're the most likely."

Arlette tooled her Porsche along the dark, wet roads with the easy competence she gave to everything she did, driving swiftly but with due regard to rain-slick surface conditions. "It doesn't make sense," she said. "A high-level service of that kind wouldn't involve itself in petty blackmail with no political, military, or industrial purpose."

"It wouldn't," I agreed. "The purpose of whichever service set up the Dhalsten operation is to gather intelligence. On and from people in sensitive positions, French and foreign. Diplomats, government functionaries, businessmen, terrorists, antiadministration political figures, scientists, etc. To keep tabs on what they're up to and to gather useful information. Probably also to catch some of them in indiscretions that can be used to exert leverage on them."

The night lights of the Côte d'Azur Airport were in sight ahead. The tails of two jumbos loomed above the palm trees bordering the end of the field.

I said, "But the upper levels of those services don't handle the day-to-day running of operations like that. Their low-level operatives do. Men like Jacques Morel."

"You think he's been giving his service everything that falls into what they want while using some of the rest of what he gets to make himself extra money on the side."

"That's what I think," I said. "Anne-Marie talked to Christian Gardier about her fear of losing her son—in that hotel. Morel could use that threat to make her keep paying him off. With what she had in her savings, at first. Then by selling her jewels and securities. Finally she didn't have

anything left to sell, except Mona Vaillant's designs—to
Serge Lotis.''

Arlette considered it briefly and shrugged. ''Everything
you've said would fit—but it's just guesswork. Nothing I
can work with. It's not evidence.''

''That's true,'' I acknowledged. ''And even good
guesses won't pry Crow out of prison. I'll have to get
more.''

''How?''

''First by finding out if my guesswork is right. That
includes finding out who Morel works with and for. I'll
have to start pushing them. Trying to make them expose
themselves, forcing them to take bigger chances.''

Arlette pulled up in front of the airport terminal, turned
to look at me, and repeated, ''How?''

''The fastest way,'' I told her, ''is for me to go have a
talk with Jacques Morel tomorrow. See if I can needle him
into coming after me. If he isn't doing that already. If he
doesn't react, my guesswork is wrong.''

She narrowed her eyes. ''If you're right—about what's
behind all this—that could be extremely dangerous for you.
I don't like it.''

''I don't much like it myself. And the more we talk
about it, the less I like it.''

''But you're going to do it anyway.''

I nodded. ''So let's drop the subject for a while.'' I put
my hand on her head and slid my fingers through the soft-
ness of her short-cropped hair. ''Do you have more work
to do tonight?''

She regarded me gravely for a moment. Then she smiled
one of those small smiles. ''Yes, I do. But I can catch up
on it in the morning.''

I got out of the Porsche, taking my overnight bag with
me. Arlette drove off. I went down to the underground

garage, got my Peugeot, and headed for the Hotel Napoleon.

Arlette was waiting for me in the small lobby, holding my room key. I took it from her, and she gave the night clerk a good night smile. I put my arm around her and drew her close as we took the elevator up to the room.

She had booked one of the Napoleon's best. The bathtub was built for two, and the bed was king-size. We found the bath a cozy fit and the bed just right.

We had always been good for each other, and we still were.

Problem-free mutual passion isn't the same as being in love. But then, nothing is. Including breaking the bank at Monte Carlo. There are some things to be said, however, for just plain feeling good—without complications.

22

I'D BEEN RIGHT about the night's change in the wind. The morning sky had been swept clean of clouds and mist. The wind was dwindling to a soft warm breeze at eight A.M. Everything outside was still glistening wet, but the sun was already at work on that. By noon the mobs would have dry beaches again.

I went to my house first. By day its potential as a trap was lessened.

Going down the drive, I stopped at the place of Bill and Judith Ruyter, a Dutch couple who were my nearest neighbors. Judith was in her garden with her two kids, picking up snails and dropping them into a shoe box. After a rain all the snails come out of their hiding places to feed. It's a good time to get them before they eat up all your plants.

Getting out of my car, I asked Judith if she and her husband had seen or heard anyone around my place last night. They hadn't. I hadn't really expected they would.

I left my car there and walked the rest of the way down with my jacket open for quick access to my gun.

Whoever might have been waiting for me at my house last night was probably gone. Day cut the chances of catching me unaware and disposing of me quietly. If it got noisy, it would be impossible for any attack party to get away unnoticed. There weren't many ways off the Lower Corniche above the drive. A phone call from any of my neighbors to the police would block those few ways.

But that didn't mean nothing was waiting for me.

I circled the house, scanning each part of my route before using it. From the patio out back there were two rear ways into the house. Both were floor-to-ceiling glass doors: one to the living room, the other into my bedroom. I peered through both and saw nothing unusual. At the living room door I put the side of my face against the glass and studied the parts inside around its edges and lock. Finally I took out one of my keys and unlocked it.

I stepped inside with the P7 in my hand. The house seemed empty. I walked through it, searching. I didn't have to search far.

It was attached to the inside of the front door at the height of my face. From it a slack wire ran to a nail hammered into the ceiling.

If I had come in that way, I would have pushed the door almost all the way open and taken a step inside when the wire pulled taught and the explosion tore me apart.

I didn't go near it. Backing away, I went through the rest of the house. There was nothing else. I went to the bedroom and packed a canvas suitcase, then carried it up the drive and put it in my car. I didn't plan on coming back to the house until this was over.

Driving back in the direction of Nice, I stopped at the Beaulieu post office and called the Cap d'Ail gendarmerie. The voice that answered was a familiar one: Adjutant Robert Ducret.

I told him about the bomb attached to the inside of my front door.

He was impressed. "I'll contact the captain at the Brigade de Recherche immediately. He'll get the army's bomb disposal experts to your place as quickly as possible."

"Tell them to go through the back door to my living room. I left it closed but not locked."

"But you will be there to meet them when they . . ."

"I can't get there right now," I told him. "I'll be in touch with you again as soon as I can."

"But—"

I hung up on him. I would have amends to make when I returned to Cap d'Ail, but that couldn't be helped.

Next I called Fritz Donhoff's apartment in Paris and brought him up to date. When I told him about the bomb he said, "These people are playing very rough, Peter. Be careful."

"You be careful," I told him. "They know a lot about me by now, and that probably includes the fact that we're partners and that you're the one I check with for most of my Paris information. If they're worried I'm finding out too much, they'll worry about what I might have told you. And you're stuck in that apartment. You'll need a bodyguard for a while."

"I appreciate your concern for me, Peter, but I am still quite capable of protecting myself."

In the war Fritz had probably killed more Nazi officials and collaborators than anyone else in the underground movement in Paris. But he was seventy-three now and had a bad leg. "*I'll* get you a bodyguard," I told him, and I hung up on his protests.

The man I phoned to take care of him was Jean-Marie Reju, a private detective in Paris who specialized in personal protection work. Before going private Reju had been with the government's V.O. service, which supplies bodyguards to foreign dignitaries visiting France and high French officials traveling abroad.

After he'd said he was available I told him enough to know what he might be up against. "These people are serious professionals. There've been three killings in less than a week that I know about. They might come after Fritz next. I want you to stick with him twenty-four hours a day. He's got a sofa in his living room that converts into a bed. And check my apartment next door now and then, just in case. Fritz has the key. And there's a secret way between his place and mine. Have him show you how it works.''

"How long is this job for?'' Reju asked.

"I don't know at this point. Not long, I hope, with what you charge.''

From Beaulieu I drove out past the airport to Cagnes-sur-Mer. Leaving my car four blocks from the Hotel Dhalsten, I walked the rest of the way. I phoned the hotel from a bistro across the street and asked for Jacques Morel. According to Captain Rinaldi, the hotel was where Morel lived as well as worked. The switchboard tried his room, got no answer, and rang his office. The man who answered there said Morel had gone out but was expected back shortly. If I would care to leave my name . . .

I didn't. I left and crossed to the hotel. The doorman was wearing the same uniform, but he wasn't the one I'd talked to a couple evenings before. Neither was the desk clerk inside. He checked his register and informed me that they did just happen to have a room available for me. He said it as if he thought I was a lucky man. I let him have a look at my American passport, paid in advance with a credit card, and explained that my luggage would arrive later. After the bellboy took his tip and left me alone in my room I looked the place over.

It was the same as hotel-chain guest rooms the world over. Spacious, comfortable, sterile. Abstract prints on the walls, TV and stereo, bar and refrigerator, three phones, including one in the bathroom. It took me several minutes to find it: a video eye, cunningly hidden in an ornamental molding that was part of the new ceiling and walls put in when the place had been renovated. It was aimed at the bed.

I didn't search for any others. Nor for bugs. I had what I'd booked the room for: confirmation that the Dhalsten's guest rooms were under electronic surveillance. Going back down to the lobby, I used one of the public phone booths to call Jacques Morel's office again. He still hadn't come back.

There was a coffee shop off the lobby, divided from it by a glass wall. I went in and sat at the counter where I could watch most of the lobby. I ordered a *café crème*, paid for it as soon as I got it, and waited.

He came into the lobby through the front entrance a few minutes later.

He was dressed in the same dark gray business suit. Long, thick body. Short, heavy legs that seemed to plant themselves briefly with each step. The hawklike beak of a nose that Captain Rinaldi had described. His dark hair, I saw now, was streaked with gray.

By the time he was two thirds of the way across the lobby I was close behind him.

"Morel," I said.

He stopped and turned to face me. He was close to fifty, with a bull-like strength to him. His broad face had been coarsened by long exposure in extreme climates, hot and cold. There were deep trenches in his cheeks. His mouth was abnormally small and thin. His eyes were pale gray. There was an instant of surprise in his expression. Then it was gone.

"No," I said, "I'm not a ghost. The bomb didn't work."

"What are you talking about?" Morel asked without emotion. "And who are you?"

"You're hurting my feelings," I said. "Forgetting my memorable television performance so soon." I gestured at one of the lobby's more obvious video cameras. "But I have the feeling we met before that. Don't you?"

He never shifted his eyes away from mine. He had a hard stare. That never varied, even when his small mouth smiled. It wasn't the stare of a man trying to impress you with how hard he was. It was his normal look, something acquired from a lifetime of dealing with violence and surviving it; of delivering violence and seeing his enemies fail to survive it.

I said, "If you don't want to talk to me . . ."

"But I do," Morel said. So far his tone hadn't varied from a flat monotone. "I have to drop by the office first, check my night staff's reports and make sure all the day crew is in."

"You're a man with heavy responsibilities."

"Yes." Morel nodded toward the coffee shop. "It will only take a few minutes. Will you wait for me?"

"Sure." I watched him walk off between the registration desk and the porter's counter and enter a door behind them.

When I went back into the coffee shop I settled into a booth and ordered a *citron pressé*. Morel, I figured, was using the time to make some quick phone calls. To associates, or employers, or underlings. Whichever, it would be to tell them where I was. Perhaps phoning wasn't necessary. They could be there in the hotel, part of his staff.

Some ten minutes went by. Morel wasn't worried I'd walk out too soon. He'd be keeping tabs on me via his closed-circuit video system. He knew I was still there—giving him time to get his men into position. They wouldn't try anything here. They'd tail me and wait until they had me someplace isolated and unobserved.

As I'd told Arlette, that was one of the things I'd come to the Dhalsten for. It was sometimes the only way to get what you needed. Provoke the enemy into making the moves. Hope they'd take chances that gave you evidence of the who and why.

It was a workable tactic, if you could survive the chances they took.

Morel came into the coffee shop and sat down facing me. He placed his powerful hands on the table, resting them on their sides, the thick, short fingers curled. His thumbs were shaped like heavy-caliber bullets—the type palmistry experts call "Murderer's Thumbs."

"Now," Morel said, "what did you want to talk about?"

"We could start with your telling me why Anne-Marie Vaillant and August Pilon had to be killed."

Morel frowned slightly, not looking away from me. He had a quiet sureness that demanded wary respect. You could hate him, but it would be stupid to underestimate him, even for a moment. A capable and dangerous man.

He said, "Tell me what reason you have to think I might be able to answer that question."

"You missed a few things when you cleaned up her apartment," I told him.

Morel didn't bite. "I'm waiting to hear why you believe I would have any interest in what you've said."

"Does your secret service know you've been using some of the stuff you tape here for your own personal blackmail operation?" I might not be able to make him bite, but I could make him wince—even if he kept it inside where I couldn't see it. "I think I'll have to discuss that with some of your superiors."

It was like trying to dig a reaction out of a block of

granite with your fingertips. His expression didn't alter. He looked at his watch and stood up. His men were where he'd told them to be now.

"I don't think you have anything to say that interests me," he said. "Good-bye."

The way he said it, the good-bye had a certain finality. He turned his back on me and marched out of the coffee shop toward the rear of the lobby.

I went out of the hotel to find out which one of us had just made the wrong decision.

23

I TURNED INLAND off the Grande Corniche onto narrow route D53. The two-lane road curled around a hump and then began skirting a series of high, rugged valleys cut off from any view of the sea.

Trees became smaller there. Tangles of wild bushes grew more dense, covering much of the terrain. Boulders and spurs of jagged rock jutted out of the green slopes. Steeper slopes became bare stone, gleaming so white in the sunlight that from a distance they seemed covered with snow. There were only occasional houses, most of them weekend places now locked up and empty. Farms were few and tiny. The soil here is spread too thin over a base of porous limestone to support much cultivation. The limestone is like a sponge: rainwater sinks into it too quickly, below where roots can reach, leaving the earth bone-dry most of the year.

Until then I hadn't worried too much about which cars were behind me. The three *corniches*, and the roads connecting them, were too full of midsummer tourist traffic to spot a tail. And any car that was after me wouldn't make its move with that many people around and traffic jams impeding swift escape.

But few tourists venture inland behind the highest *corniche*. If they can't see the Mediterranean, they don't believe they're on the Riviera.

Routes like the D53 are used by residents of the coast

who like to dine in high backcountry villages with cooler air and fewer vacation mobs. But that is mostly on weekends. During the week these roads are virtually empty.

In the first four miles after leaving the Grande Corniche I met only two vehicles coming the other way. One was an aged Volkswagen filled with as much family as could be jammed into it. The other was one of the big construction trucks that brought sand and stones down from the quarries that are the only industry in that area.

There were three cars behind me. The closest was a white two-door Audi Quatro with a license plate ending in 06, the number for the local Alpes Maritimes department. There was nobody in it except the driver. It wasn't likely Morel would have sent only one man to take me out.

Behind the Audi was a four-door blue Fiat. There were two people in it, but I couldn't make out if they were both men or a man and a woman. And I couldn't read its dirt-smeared license.

The third car was a tan Citroën Turbo, the very fast version the manufacturers named "The Demon". There were two people in the front seat, and it was the best candidate for a car intended to stick with me and eventually overhaul me. But it was too far back. There were long curves in the road where it didn't have me in sight for as long as a minute. Long enough for me to detour into a dirt side road without its spotting the move.

Any of the three cars could be my tail. Or none of them. Morel could have decided on a different way of getting rid of me. Or his tail car could have lost me in the traffic coming up from the coast. Or . . .

I slowed down, bringing the white Audi up closer. Its driver appeared to be wearing some kind of lumber jacket. I couldn't make out his face, but the shape of his head and the girth of his shoulders were like Jacques Morel's. That wasn't likely. I didn't see how he could have gotten out of his hotel and into a car close behind me before I'd driven out of Cagnes-sur-Mer. And the practical consideration still held. If you intend to overtake and attack another car, the professional technique is one man driving and a second man holding a weapon ready.

The Audi slowed down before it could get any closer. Then it slowed more, increasing the gap between us. Possibly a nervous driver who didn't approve of tailgating. The horn of the Fiat behind him blared angrily. The Audi pulled over and let it pass. That brought the Fiat close enough for me to see that its license plate was local. The people in it were a man and a woman. Women killers are not unknown. I accelerated, getting further ahead again. I didn't intend to let any of those cars pull up alongside me.

A couple miles further on there was a sharp turnoff from the D53 onto a narrower road, the D22. I took the turnoff. The D22 climbed straight for about six yards and then hair-pinned in the other direction, still climbing. When I was around the turn I slowed my Peugeot almost to a halt and looked down to my left. The Fiat stuck to the D53, going on past the turnoff toward the village of Peille. The white Audi followed it slowly. The tan Citroën Demon turned up onto the D22 after me.

I accelerated, following the tight bends of the mountain road. It kept twisting its way upward, snaking towards the three-thousand-foot-high Col de la Madonna, a pass across the summits of this mountain chain.

In every direction now the view was cut off abruptly by rising cliffs, peaks, ridges. There were no houses at all in sight anymore.

The road grew much narrower. In places it was only a bit wider than my car. If two cars met, the one descending was supposed to back up until it reached a wider point where it could pull over and let the climbing car pass. But there were no cars coming down toward me. Only the one behind.

It came into sight on a short straight stretch. Close enough to see the two people in it were both men. Close enough to read its license plate. It ended with the number 75—a car from Paris.

It began gaining on me, but not for long. I twisted around another hairpin and it was lost to sight back there. The Citroën was a faster car than my Peugeot. On a straight road it would have caught up to me. But the D22 has a very few straight stretches. Most of it is one hairpin turn after another. The Citroën had trouble with bends that tight. My car did not. I'd done alot of work on it, making it ready for mountain road rallies.

After Attilio Bettega had crashed to his death in the last Tour of Corsica I'd pulled out of that rally and begun considering giving up rally driving entirely. But I still had experience with roads like this one, and I had a car capable of handling it. If that had been my aim, I could have reached the Col de la Madonna far ahead of the pursuing Citroën. But I didn't want to lose the men in it. I wanted information from them.

The road got steeper and tougher. In places it couldn't get around the massive outcroppings of rock and had to go under them, via short, rough-cut tunnels. After each turn the sides of the narrow road changed. The slope rising steeply from one edge of the road would be on my right, and the one dropping below the other side on my left—and then, abruptly, the upslope would be on my left and the downslope on my right. The higher the road climbed the more savage the slopes became, with more of the rock showing its teeth through the heavy underbrush, and sharp stones on the road where there had been slides.

Three miles above the point where I'd turned onto the D22, just below the Col de la Madonna, a side road cut away from it up to my right. As soon as the Citroën came in sight I turned up this side road.

It had no official route number. Once it had been a military road leading to underground bunkers atop the mountain. The bunkers had been locked up long ago. The road remained, but it dead-ended in the middle of nowhere. It was used only by occasional small-game hunters now. There were signs beside the road warning that it was forbidden to hunt in this area. Each sign was riddled with bullet holes. The French have a contempt for laws that can't be enforced.

I heard the powerful engine of the Citroën behind me, increasing speed to catch up. This was a good place for them to finish with me. Nobody around to see or hear. Even if a rare passing motorist did hear gunfire here, it would be assumed that it was the shots of hunters and would be ignored.

But the old military road was perfect for my purpose, too. And I probably knew it better than they did. I gunned the Peugeot's engine and squealed around its tight turns, always climbing, staying far enough ahead as I neared the place I wanted.

I drove around a long hairpin bend, stopped the Peugeot on the other side of it, and jumped out. A cliff formed a wall along the left-hand side of the road. I climbed down off the road on the right-hand side. I had to place each step cautiously. The two days of rain had washed earth away from the roadside and the slopes below it, exposing loose stones and shards of broken rock.

I turned to face the road behind a screen of scrub brush

and then hunkered down, holding the P7 ready in both hands and listening to the oncoming Citroën.

The driver wouldn't see my car blocking the way until he came around the bend. With no way around the Peugeot, he would have to brake to a very sharp halt to avoid crashing into it. That would stop the Citroën directly in front of me, with the busy driver on the other side. The man holding the gun would be on my side. When I straightened up I would be aiming my gun straight through the car window at his head, at a distance of about ten inches.

That was the way it should have worked. It would have, except the Citroën came around the bend much too fast, tires squealing, and skidded on gravel on the road. The driver and his partner had gotten too eager to catch me. When he saw my car dead ahead the driver practically stood on his brakes. That made the Citroën skid worse, out of control—in my direction.

The roadside had been undermined by the rain. When the weight of the heavy car skidded onto it the roadside collapsed. The Citroën slid off the road and down the slope toward me.

I leapt out of its way. Stones rolled under my feet, and I fell, landing awkwardly on my side. Reaching out quickly with my left hand, I grabbed the base of a spreading juniper bush and stopped myself from sliding further. Tightening my right-hand grip on the pistol, I watched the Citroën go down the slope past me.

It started the whole slope sliding after it: dirt, rock, and bushes. My juniper went with it, and so did I. The knuckles of my right fist cracked sharply across a rock, springing my fingers open. The P7 flew out of my hand.

An instant later I had both feet braced against the trunk of a hip-high hermes oak, stopping my slide. Close below me the Citroën tilted over on two wheels and began to

topple. The man beside the driver kicked open his door
and started to jump out. The heavy car crashed over on its
side on top of him.

It continued to roll over on its roof and then came to a
halt lying on its other side. The man who'd jumped out lay
broken on the ground, a short-barreled pump-action shotgun in the dirt near his lifeless hands.

The driver appeared, climbing up out of the overturned
car. His cheek was bleeding, but other than that he seemed
undamaged. He was a squat man with apelike arms. His
jacket was open, and I could see he was wearing a shoulder
harness. But there was nothing in its holster or in his hands.
He'd lost his gun somewhere inside the car.

I was on my feet by then and looking for my own gun.
I spotted it lying beside a tangle of buckthorn and wild
strawberry bushes. But there was no time left to go for it.
The squat driver was out of the Citroën and dashing toward
the fallen shotgun. He was snatching it up with one hand
when I did the only thing I could. I jumped and landed on
him, ramming him to the ground under me.

The shotgun jumped from his hand and skittered away
from us. I surged to my feet to go after it. He came up just
as fast and clouted me across the back of my skull, knock-
ing me back down. I kicked his ankles out from under him
and he fell over on me, away from the shotgun.

He locked his hands around my neck and dug his thumbs
into my throat. I shoved both forearms up under his jaw to
force his head back and make him let go. He was enor-
mously strong. His thumbs didn't dig in deeper, but he
didn't let go. We rolled over a couple times, away from
the shotgun, fetching up against a boulder.

I rammed the heel of my left hand against the base of
his nose, smacking his head against the boulder. His grip
on my throat loosened, and I struck at his throat with the

edge of my right hand. He sideslipped the blow and scrambled to his feet. I scrambled to mine. He crouched a little, fists cocked, left foot pointing toward me and right foot braced a bit behind, neatly balanced. He had the battered face of an ex-boxer. But I wasn't going to box with him.

I bent forward and rushed him, head down. A fist glanced off the back of my head, and then I had him trapped against the boulder and was working in close, bringing my knee up into his groin, and kidney–punching him at the same time.

He groaned but didn't go down. And he knew dirty infighting, too. He tried to smash my instep with the heel of his shoe. I avoided it, but that gave him a little room between us. One of his hands grabbed my ear to yank my head forward while his other hand drove two stiffened fingers at my eyes.

I twisted against the grip on my ear, and the fingers struck my forehead. I caught one of them in my right hand and bent it all the way back and heard it snap. He screamed and yanked the injured hand away from me, trying to get further away, but he was stopped by the boulder. I chopped him across the throat while he was trying and hit the target this time.

He made a gagging noise and reached up with both arms when I feinted another strike at his throat. I hit him in the belly. Three times, as hard as I could and very low: left, right, left.

He sagged to his knees, arms hanging to the ground, head lolling. He wasn't out—but he was finished. I crouched in front of him. He tried to say something, but the pressure of blood pounding inside my ears made it impossible for me to hear him. Taking slow breaths to bring the pressure down, I went through his pockets looking for identity papers.

I hadn't found anything when he started talking again. This time I could make out his thick whisper:

"We'll get you . . . traitor."

I stared at him. "Traitor? To what?"

"France . . ."

"I can't be," I told him. "I'm not French. I'm American."

He peered at me blearily. "But . . . he said . . ."

Before I could ask who he was talking about, he was no longer looking at me. He was looking at something behind and above me. It was an old trick, but I was sure he was in no condition to pull it off. So I turned to look.

A rifle cracked from the road above.

The bullet ripped the front of my shirt and burned across my chest.

24

IT COULD HAVE been worse. Like being dead instead of stung. If I hadn't turned in that instant, the shot would have broken my spine. As it was, it only gouged some of my skin away—before smashing through the ribcage of the man I'd been questioning and entering his heart.

I was sprinting away around the boulder when he slumped over on the ground. Another rifle shot kicked up dirt between my legs just before I swung behind the protection of the boulder.

I stayed there, crouched and breathing hard again, for a few seconds. Then I went flat on the ground and snaked to the other side of the boulder. Staying low, I edged my head forward just enough to squint one eye up at the road.

A white car was up there at the turn of the bend. The man standing beside it with the rifle, wearing a lumber jacket, was Jacques Morel.

That was how they'd stayed close enough, when I was driving up through traffic, to tail me without my spotting it. Morel in the white Audi and the other two in the Citroën, taking turns coming near and dropping back. The two cars in radio contact.

Morel raised his rifle and took aim at me. I ducked back just in time. The bullet *spang*ed off the edge of the boulder, almost exactly where my head had been, chopping off chips of stone. He couldn't possibly have seen that small part of my face from his position up there. He'd just guessed where I'd be.

That made him a very good guesser. I'd have to do some smart calculating of my own to get to him or away from him. I preferred trying to get to him first. But he had that rifle, and I didn't have anything.

The shotgun was nearest. But it was out in the open. I'd never live to get near it, against a marksman like Morel.

My own gun was further away. I might be able to get to it, however, using cover all the way. If I could, a handgun still wouldn't be any good at that range against a rifle. But it wasn't a shooting match I was after. Because I had two big problems at that point.

The first problem, naturally, was staying alive. The second was allied to that and almost as important: Morel wanted to kill me—but I didn't want to kill him. Dead, he was no use to me. If he died now, the truth died with him. My guesses would stay guesses, and Crow would stay in prison. I needed Morel alive to get information out of him, one way or another.

If I could get my handgun, the object would be to try circling around behind his position and then to get in close to his back. Once I had the drop on him we'd find out if he could be forced to talk. I doubted it, but it was worth a try.

Whether I *could* get close behind him depended on whether he was as good at stalking in this kind of terrain as I was.

We'd see.

Keeping low, with the boulder giving cover between me and Morel, I went down into a low forest of bramble, stubby spruce trees, mastic, and juniper. My gun was off to the left and about twenty yards further up the slope. I went left through the forest, my route diverging slightly whenever necessary to avoid forcing my way through tangles of bushes that would give my movements away.

I went past the point where my pistol was waiting above. A few yards further on I found what I was hunting for: one of the trenches cut into the slope by runoffs of the rains. Downrushing water always seeks the easiest route, gouging out soft earth and loose stones, twisting its way around and between harder concentrations of rock.

Using a clump of nettles as cover, I slipped into the trench and began crawling upward through it. It wasn't deep, but as long as I stayed on my hands and knees it would shelter me. Whether it would also conceal me was another matter. The rains had been recent, but the trench was already bone dry. It was bottomed with a carpet of crumbled clay and fine grains of sand. There was no way to climb it without raising some dust.

A *little* dust shouldn't give away my position. It was unlikely Morel would be able to spot it from up there on the road.

I reached the height where I judged my gun had fallen—and kept climbing the trench. There wasn't sufficient cover outside the trench there. A little further up there would be.

I was almost there when Morel's rifle sounded again. The bullet slashed into the side of the trench a few inches above my back, showering me with dirt and pebbles.

The shot hadn't come from up on the road. Morel had climbed down to find me. He'd spotted that little bit of dust stirred up by my crawl. And he'd pinpointed my position exactly.

Now I knew: He *was* good at this kind of stalk.

But his judgment of how to use his advantage was dubious. Morel still couldn't see me—just my position. He had tried for a lucky shot. Hoping the bullet would ricochet and hit me. Or scare me into jumping into his sights. He was anxious to finish me quickly. That can cloud a stalk-er's tactical decisions.

His error told me where he was: off to the left of my trench. That was fine, my gun was off to the right. I resumed my crawling climb. Raising more dust. He didn't waste another shot. Probably Morel was climbing, too. Aiming to get up near where the trench flattened out so he could have a clear shot at me when I reached that point.

But I didn't go that high. I stopped when I reached a place where screens of high bushes almost met across the top of the trench. With that for cover I eased out on my belly. I snaked under the bushes to my right and looked down the slope.

From there I could see the bushes below that concealed my gun. There was open space between them and the ones under which I lay. Speed would be the only cover across that space. And surprise: He was expecting me to continue trying to get to high ground, not back down.

I got my feet under me and dove out of my screen, straight down toward the bushes below. I hit the ground on one shoulder and did a fast roll through those bushes with thorns scratching and tugging at me. Then I was through them—and there was my gun. As I grabbed it Morel fired through the bushes at me. The bullet whipped past my ear.

No error on his part this time. The bushes concealed me but didn't protect me. If he kept firing through them, one of the shots was bound to hit me. If I stayed put.

I fired three fast shots at his position. Blind shots, to drive him to cover and give myself a half second's grace while I jumped for the trench. It worked. I fell inside the trench and lay flat in the bottom for a moment. No longer. The object now was to keep things moving and changing rapidly, not giving Morel time to rethink his plans.

A few large stones had fallen into the trench with me. I chose the two roundest and sent them rolling down the trench. They raised as much dust as my crawling had. While Morel's eyes would be following that down, I went up.

When I reached my screen of bushes I again slipped out of the trench under them. This time I didn't pause there. I snaked away to the right, angling upward. On that part of the slope the *maquis*—the dense conglomeration of stumpy trees and high brush—spread for over forty yards. I kept to its cover until I reached a place where rocky spurs jutted out of the slope. Climbing around the nearest spur, I stopped to scrutinize the area where Morel had last been heard from.

There was no sign of him. I reined in my nerves and kept scanning that area, up and down. Finally I detected a stirring of some bushes there. No wind was blowing. The movement could only be Morel.

It was too far for precision shooting with a handgun. And I still had the same problem. I couldn't chance killing him. Killing me was his objective. He had a rifle that outranged my weapon, and by then I knew he was too good for me to get close before he knew it. Another notion gone awry.

Another tangle of bushes stirred slightly. Morel was working his way back up toward the road. But I was closer to it than him now. I went the rest of the way swiftly, keeping the spurs of rock between me and Morel.

I pulled myself onto the road and stayed low until I reached my car. Crouching, I went around it to the driver's side and slid in behind the wheel.

As I gunned away Morel fired again. The bullet pierced my rear window and went out the left side window behind me. The next second I was around another tight bend, out of his line of vision. Those who run away live to connive another day.

Morel's Audi had little hope of catching my souped-up Peugeot on roads like this. I doubted he'd make the attempt. He'd missed his try here, and, like me, he'd be thinking out alternative methods.

My own drive up into these hills hadn't been entirely fruitless. I had the Paris license number of that Citroën. And I knew the two men in it had thought they were coming to kill a French traitor. That made them something other than hired hoodlums, which had been a possibility until then.

Near the mountain summit, shortly before the place where the military road ended at the closed-down bunkers, a wide dirt-and-gravel path cut away from it. I drove onto the path, following its curling route over a hump and down another slope. That took me back to route D22, beyond the point where I'd left it, on the other side of the Col de la Madonna.

After that pass through the mountains the D22 begins to descend, via more gradual turns, in the direction of the sea. Seven miles of it brought me to the village of Sainte Agnès, perched on a hilltop at an altitude of two thousand feet and reputedly the highest town in Europe with a view of the sea. Cutting below the village, I drove down to Menton, the last French city before the Italian border. I used its main post office to phone Fritz Donhoff.

"Is Reju there?" I asked him.

"Yes," Fritz told me sourly. "If he is the one you wish to speak to . . ."

"No, I just want to be sure he's with you. The situation's likely to get rougher now."

"If it does," Fritz said with a heavy sarcasm intended

for his temporary bodyguard, "Reju need not fear. I will protect him."

I gave him the license number of the Citroën from Paris. "Get me something on its owner as soon as you can. I'll be up there to do the legwork."

"When are you coming?"

"By this evening," I told him.

"I'll have it for you by then."

I was sure he would. Fritz's contact in the vehicle control branch of the Paris police enjoyed the magnums of champagne that came his way without fail every Christmas, Easter, and New Year.

⊠ 25 ⊠

My PLANE LANDED at Orly ten minutes after seven that evening. It was still bright day—and hot. A thick heat that made my light chest bandage itch. Morel's bullet had only grazed me, but risk of infection made it wisest to tolerate the bandage, and the ointment under it, for a couple of days.

I didn't give my apartment address to the cabdriver. Instead I told him to take me to a parking garage a couple blocks from it.

When you travel by air the difficulty of getting a gun through boarding control can sometimes be a problem for someone in my business. I had left the P7 behind, tucked in its hidden compartment inside the rear seat of the Peugeot. More of Jacques Morel's people could have the street outside my apartment staked out. I needed another weapon before approaching it.

The taxi carried me into a Paris full of foreigners and half-emptied of Parisians. Two thirds of the shops, restaurants, and cafés were closed for four to six weeks. Summer is when Paris gets the most visitors, so that's when the city's merchants *could* make the most money. That doesn't matter to them; tradition dictates that they close up and go away. For Parisians, a long midsummer holiday, preferably down on the Riviera, is sacrosanct.

My apartment, and the garage where I kept my car, were near Place Contrescarpe. One of the oldest quarters of

Paris, now popular again as a mixed-income family neighborhood. Workers, merchants, and members of the professions. Students from the nearby universities and kids going to local nursery and grade schools. Retired folks regarded as the elders of the community. And the *clochards*, a small group of Paris bums who still consider Place Contrescarpe home base and are tolerated as a vestige of old traditions.

The garage was on Rue de l'Estrapade, a block behind the Panthéon. My three-year-old Renault 5 was on the third level. I unlocked it but didn't drive it out. Open-air parking is hard to find before midnight in the narrow streets of that quarter.

I climbed into the rear of the car and reached up under the back seat. As with the Peugeot in the south, I'd rigged a hidden compartment inside it.

This one held a stubby Mauser. A good tight-corner defense weapon. I holstered it under my jacket and slipped a spare ammo clip in my pocket. Then I relocked the Renault and walked the two blocks to Place Contrescarpe carrying my lightweight canvas suitcase.

The adjacent apartments Fritz and I had bought before neighborhood prices went up were in one of the solid restored houses inside a small courtyard half a block from the *place*, on Rue Lacépède. I checked out the street as I walked through it. Most of the people in sight I knew. None of those I didn't recognize seemed to be paying undue attention to my address.

The courtyard was inside a tall wooden fence that concealed it from the street. I pressed the buzzer button beside its door. That clicked the lock open and simultaneously turned on two lamps in the courtyard. The lamps operated day and night. By day you didn't notice their light, but at night it was useful. The courtyard cobbles were uneven—

easy to trip on in the dark, especially for women and cowboys with high heels.

I went into the courtyard carrying the suitcase in my left hand, my right free for the Mauser if necessary. It wasn't necessary. I circled the tall plane tree in the center of the court without incident, entered the house, and climbed the stairs. There was a short landing on the second floor. The door to my apartment was on one side, Fritz Donhoff's on the other. I rang his bell and announced who I was through the door.

Jean-Marie Reju let me in. He was holding a Colt .45 in his long, skinny hand. Not pointing it at me, just holding it. Reju was a rangy man of thirty, wide-shouldered but lean. He wore his sandy hair in a crew cut. Thick glasses made his watchful eyes look tiny. When he was sure that it was me and that nobody else was behind me Reju stood aside so I could enter. He didn't smile at me, though we'd known each other for some years. I'd never seen him laugh. Life was a deadly serious business for Reju. His only relationships seemed to be with the people he protected. A lonely man, but good at his work. When I was inside he shut and relocked the door. Not until then did he stick the .45 back in his hip holster.

I put down my suitcase and looked at Fritz. He was a big, heavy, dignified man with baggy eyes and silvery hair. Seated behind the living room table in a wheeled, leather-padded swivel chair with his injured leg up on a footstool. He looked as neat as always. His trousers were recently pressed, his fresh shirt was buttoned, and his necktie was held just so with a pearl stickpin. He opened his arms with a warm smile of welcome. I went over and bent to hug him.

He thumped me on the back fondly. "Good to see you,

my boy, good to see you. Especially after being shut up in here with this zombie.''

"Where are your local ladies?'' I asked him.

"Oh, they drop by. But *he* chases them away.''

Reju frowned at him. "You want them around if somebody starts shooting? Or tosses a bomb?''

"You're right,'' Fritz admitted grudgingly. "If only you weren't so damn boring.''

Reju was not offended. He acted like a veteran nurse dealing with a cranky patient.

I gestured at the chess game in progress on the table. "Who's winning?'' It was the middle game, and at that point Fritz had lost two pawns to take one of Reju's knights.

"He's a terrible player,'' Fritz complained.

"So far,'' Reju said in that humorless voice, "I've won three games to your one.''

"Because you take so long to make each move!'' Fritz growled. "It makes me nervous.''

"And *you* move too quickly,'' Reju told him. "Chess requires time to think.'' He walked over to the living room window to scan the courtyard below.

I asked when he'd last checked out my apartment.

"Fifteen minutes ago,'' Reju said, and he walked off through Fritz's apartment to have a look through the back windows.

Fritz picked his Beretta 92SB pistol off the seat beside him and placed it on the table near the chessboard. I had a gun just like it hidden in my own apartment. I sat down in the chair and asked, "What have you got for me?''

"A number of items. First of all, that Paris license number. The Citroën belongs to Paul Orain. Known in the *milieu* as the Butterfly, because he has a large tattoo of one on his chest. Known to the police as a professional thug.

A contract leg-breaker. Possibly also a killer, though that has never been proved. Definitely a dealer in *blanche* as well. He's done time for that.''

Blanche is police argot for heroin. "Did you get a description of him?" I asked Fritz.

"Naturally." The man he described sounded like the ape who'd driven the Citroën and been killed by the bullet Morel had intended for me.

"This Paul Orain," Fritz said, "lived in the quarter between the Gare du Nord and Gare de l'Est until a couple years ago. His driver's license and other papers still have that address. So far I haven't found anyone who knows where he lives now."

"He doesn't," I told Fritz. "He's dead."

"Ah. In that case, people of the *milieu* will feel freer to discuss him. There is a bar in that quarter popular with the *milieu*. The couple who own it have been friends of mine a long time. Monique and Eric Barril."

"I know them and their bar," I said. "You introduced me to them there about four years ago."

"So Monique reminded me. Orain used to frequent their place until he moved away, though she and Eric know him only as the Butterfly. She was reluctant to speak about him over the bar's phone, since it is frequently tapped by the police. As you were due in Paris and they don't close the bar until three in the morning, I didn't ask them to come here for a talk. I told Monique to expect you."

"I'll drop in around nine-thirty," I said. "The early evening crowd there has thinned out by then, and the *milieu* characters haven't started settling in for the night."

Jean-Marie Reju came back into the living room, putting on an oversized raincoat that concealed the big, long-barreled Colt on his hip. In his case it wasn't the police he was hiding it from. Reju was one of the few who could get a carry permit whenever required—without time-wasting red tape—because of his special line of work and his impeccable record with the government's V.O. department.

"I'm going to take a turn around the block." He got out one of Fritz's spare keys and used it, after he went out, to relock the door behind him.

Fritz gazed after him angrily. "Why don't you send him to protect your mother? She could be in danger, too, if . . ."

"Not necessary. She's out of the country." Her second husband was at a shipping conference in Japan, and Babette had gone with him to look at religious artworks in some of the Buddhist monasteries. I asked Fritz, "Nothing on Jacques Morel yet?"

"Very little. It's puzzling. There is no record of his existence until a few months before he went to work at the Hotel Dhalsten. And nothing since that you don't already know. He has deep cover from upper level, that is obvious."

I nodded. "Otherwise there'd be something on him, even if he's changed his name. Anything new on Serge Lotis?"

"Exactly what we were looking for," Fritz said. "His secretary checked her office calendar and notebooks for me. A delightful woman. Lotis met with Anne-Marie three months before his couture show. Just three days before he changed all his designs for it. He worked everybody day and night after that to get the collection ready on time. And he had *all* the designs already prepared for it from the moment he began the changes."

"Normally," I said, "a designer comes up with a collection bit by bit, over a long period."

"His staff thinks some unknown free-lance designer must have come in and sold the entire new line to Lotis."

"Anne-Marie. Not much question of that anymore."

"There's more," Fritz said. "Last Wednesday, after the meeting with Pilon that upset him so much, Lotis made that long-distance call to Nice." He got a slip of paper from his pocket.

I looked at the phone number he'd jotted on it. "That's Anne-Marie's private line, in her apartment workroom."

"Lotis called to warn her about Pilon. Legally, he didn't have too much to worry about—as long as he could persuade her to deny any accusation and say nothing else. He was only in danger if she broke down and admitted selling him Mona Vaillant's collection."

Fritz and I never had difficulty communicating. We thought along the same lines. "But his call only frightened her more than she was probably already frightened," I said. "It scared her into contacting Morel and—"

"How?" Fritz interrupted. "Blackmailers don't give their addresses and phone numbers to their victims."

"*They* do the contacting," I conceded. "When they want more money. How she got in touch with Morel is one point I don't have an answer to yet. But the rest fits: Anne-Marie told Morel that Pilon was getting too close to what she'd done. And Morel was forced to do something to blank out that line of inquiry."

"It may," Fritz put in, "have been the first Morel *knew* about her selling those designs to Lotis. A blackmailer doesn't ask where a victim gets the money."

"If he *had* known, he wouldn't like it. Pirating that whole collection was bound to get her in trouble if Mona launched a professional investigation."

"So when Morel did learn what she'd done, *he* got frightened."

"August Pilon had a tough reputation in our area, Fritz. If he squeezed her, she'd have ended up telling him why she needed the money. And Morel would be in worse trouble than just being charged with blackmail."

Fritz nodded thoughtfully. "He would be dead. His employers wouldn't risk his being brought to trial and exposing their illegal operation at the Hotel Dhalsten. As well as exposing that they'd been stupid in their choice of employees."

"No secret service likes that kind of scandal."

"Indeed they do not. Cabinet ministers have fallen for less."

Not only ministers. The SDECE—France's main foreign intelligence service for thirty-five years—had ceased to exist a few years before because of similar embarrassments.

Fritz said, "That *would* explain the extreme measures Jacques Morel has resorted to in order to clamp a lid on the situation."

It did explain it. But it didn't solve my problem: what to do about it. What Arlette had pointed out remained unchanged. I still didn't have anything that would get Crow out of prison.

"Are you having dinner with us?" Fritz asked me. "One of the ladies prepared an immense amount of stew."

"If you're eating soon."

"All I have to do is heat it." Fritz lifted his swollen ankle off the stool and wheeled himself swiftly across the room, propelling the swivel chair with his good foot and keeping the other raised. I followed him to the kitchen. There was a large pot waiting on the stove. Fritz turned on the burner under it and set the flame on low. As he took off the lid and stirred inside with a soup spoon there was a tantalizing aroma of boeuf Bourguignon.

Reju returned from his prowl around the block. When he saw me still there he said, "I can check out your place again if . . ."

"I'll do it." I went and picked up my suitcase. As I carried it toward the rear of Fritz's apartment Reju sat down at the chessboard and told Fritz, "It's still your move. . . ."

The back of the clothes closet in Fritz's bedroom had a secret door to my own bedroom closet. I used it and stood for a few seconds listening. My apartment seemed empty. I put the suitcase on the bed and went through the rest of the rooms with the Mauser ready. It wasn't needed.

I tucked it back in its holster and put through a call to Gilles in Nice. "Got that stuff I asked for?"

"Photostats of Anne-Marie's checks and her Visa statements," he said. "But the rest of the credit firms will take much longer to send their copies. American Express, Diners . . ."

"Send me what you have," I told him. "I'm in Paris. Arrange for a courier service to bring it up on an early flight tomorrow morning. When you know which flight let me know, and I'll be at the airport to pick it up." He already had my apartment number. I told him to leave the message on my answering machine if I was out when he phoned.

I had dinner with Fritz and Reju and then went to the garage for my car. I drove it across Paris to see if the fallen Butterfly had left anything of his past behind.

Like a crowbar I could use to pry up the truth in some form that I could work with.

"BUTTERFLY USED TO come in almost every night for years," Monique Barril said. "He'd hang around, talk big with the other *milieu* hooligans, kid around with the *poules* that came in to take the weight off their feet for a while." She gave me a defensive look. "We don't let the girls dredge for customers in here. For that they've got to go back out on the sidewalk."

"I know that," I assured her.

The bar was on the Rue des 2 Gares, with the Gare du Nord a block away in one direction and the Gare de l'Est the same short distance in another. With hordes of daily travelers pouring in and out of both stations, the area was a natural for pickpockets, purse snatchers, con men, and hookers.

As I'd expected, the bar wasn't doing heavy business at that hour. The nighttime regulars wouldn't start drifting in before eleven. Monique Barril and I were in a back booth, with nobody close to us. I had a cognac, and she was drinking tap beer. She was a fat woman with a face like a pudding. According to Fritz, she'd been a slim and pretty woman when she'd been a prostitute. She'd deliberately let herself go when she quit the trade, to prove she had no further interest in attracting men.

"Well," she said, "what can I tell you? The Butterfly, he'd hang around here for an hour or so. Drink too much.

Boast too much. Then wander out to do . . . whatever he did for a living.''

''I hear he dealt in the *blanche* and handled strong-arm jobs.''

Monique Barril nodded. ''I heard things like that, too.''

''And he sometimes took contracts to kill people,'' I added.

''That I don't know about,'' she said carefully.

There were two men in a booth up front. They looked like workers who'd finished their day but weren't in a mood to go home. Two more people were on bar stools. One was an alcoholic somewhere in his late twenties, leaning on the bar and taking small, frequent sips from a tall glass of red wine. The other was a street prostitute taking a break.

Eric Barril was behind the bar giving her some business advice. She listened with attentive respect to every word. He was twenty years older than Monique Barril. Skinny bald, with a permanently anxious face. He'd been known as Grandpop even back when he'd been Monique's pimp, before they got married.

Theirs wasn't an unusual story in France. His function as a pimp had consisted mainly of saving the money she earned. When they had saved enough they'd married and bought the bar. Other local merchants treated Monique Barril with respect, though they knew her background. Being a prostitute is not a criminal act in France. They treated her husband with less respect. Being a pimp *is* a criminal act.

Their not being considered criminals is one reason fewer French prostitutes are on drugs than those in other countries. They stay in the business only to get enough cash together to buy a small business. Most of them think they have a future. Some do, if they've been intelligent in choosing their men.

"You don't have to be careful of what you say about the Butterfly," I reminded Monique Barril. "I told you, he's dead."

When she smiled deep dimples appeared in her plump face. "I would tell you about him anyway. Any friend of Fritz . . ."

"Did this Butterfly ever mention a man named Jacques Morel?"

She thought about it and then shook her head. "No. I never heard of anybody with that name."

"Sure?"

"Sure. I've got a good memory."

I described Morel, but she couldn't remember ever having seen the Butterfly with a man who looked like that.

"What sorts of things did Butterfly boast about?" I asked her.

"Oh, the usual. How big a man he was. How much money he made. All his big connections."

"Mob connections?"

"Naturally. To hear him talk, he was close friends with every top gang leader in France. Claimed he knew big shots in the SDECE, too."

I sat up straighter. "Did he ever claim to *work* for the SDECE?"

"That's what he *said*. But a lot of those petty hoods say they work for the secret services. Saying it doesn't mean it's true."

It's the same the world over. German thugs claim they do jobs for the BND. Florida thugs boast of connections with the CIA. It's good for their prestige with other thugs.

But sometimes it's true. Secret services do have uses for men like that. As informers. And as men of violence, to carry out jobs they don't want traced back to the government.

Hoodlums who get that kind of work are proud of it. It makes them patriots, and they take that seriously.

Morel had told the Butterfly I was a traitor, and he'd had reason to believe it.

"How long has it been since you've seen the Butterfly?" I asked Monique Barril.

"Oh, about two years, I'd say."

"The SDECE was put out to pasture more than three years ago. Now it's the DGSE that handles foreign intelligence. Did he ever claim to work for the DGSE?"

"No. Other men that hang out here sometimes say they do. But never Butterfly. He was indignant about what happened to the *old* secret service. The SDECE. He used to say it was traitors inside the government that pulled it down."

I drove from the bar to one of the new condominiums springing up near La Defense. Thierry Gallion lived there with his family. He was the next logical source to try after what Monique Barril had just told me.

Detective work, private or police, depends more on who you know than on how smart you are. Without a plenitude of sources—official, criminal, and in the straight world— you're just floundering through a dark swamp without boots or a compass. Sources are your stock in trade; the more you have the better you are at your trade.

Having Fritz Donhoff as my partner had enlarged my circle of sources immensely. But I had brought to the partnership a number of my own. Some held delicate positions—above ground or down inside its rat holes—and were wary of opening up except to me personally.

Captain Thierry Gallion was one of these. He was in a peculiar position: in a rat hole, but above ground. Doubly delicate.

His father was a retired admiral. During World War II his father had been a young lieutenant, second officer of a destroyer stuck in the naval harbor of Toulon with the rest of the French fleet because of a treaty between the Vichy government and Hitler Germany. Then Hitler had broken the agreement without warning and sent an SS Panzer Korps to seize the fleet. The grab failed when most of the fleet scuttled itself at the last moment. Thierry's father had slipped out of Toulon and joined the Resistance, rejoining the navy only after the Liberation.

Former Resistance members form a tight fraternity in France. Thierry's father and my mother became friends during Resistance gatherings, and Thierry and I became friends through them.

Thierry's own career as a ship's officer had ended when the submarine he'd commanded sank to the bottom of the Pacific because of engine failure. By the time the engine was repaired bad air and depth pressure had done permanent damage to his heart and hearing. After that he'd been made a desk officer—in the SDECE.

The government's disbanding of the SDECE a few years back had consisted mainly of changing its name. Now it was the DGSE, doing exactly the same kind of intelligence and counterintelligence jobs. Some of the old officers had been dropped, but not many. Thierry commanded the same desk for the DGSE as he had for the SDECE.

He wasn't home when I reached his apartment. His wife was watching television after having put their three kids to bed. She told me Thierry was working late and asked me in for a drink.

I had one with her. Just one. Thierry's wife was pleasingly plump, well-bred, and devoted to him. But one of his less attractive sides was an unreasonable jealousy about any man she saw alone. Frenchmen are not as sexually secure as advertised.

I tore a page from my small notebook and wrote two names on it: Jacques Morel and Paul Orain, the Butterfly. Giving the paper to her, I said, "Tell Thierry I *have* to know about these men. I'll contact him at lunchtime tomorrow. He should be able to get something on them by then, if they're anywhere in the files."

I left the apartment with nothing further I could do to pursue that lead until the next day. Dropping into the nearest café, I looked up the phone number of the woman Gilles had been seeing in Paris and called her.

"Gilles warned me by phone that you might come to question me," Jacqueline Crozet said. "He told me if you did I should slam the door in your face."

"But you didn't."

"No. Gilles considers you his oldest and closest friend, Monsieur Sawyer. In spite of your not feeling too friendly toward each other at the moment. Gilles doesn't have many friends. If he and I ever do marry, you and I would be seeing each other." She smiled and shrugged. "Slamming a door in your face would not be the best beginning for *our* future relationship."

We sat facing each other across the coffee table in her living room. It was a small, pleasant room. Old, comfortable, tasteful furnishings. A lot of books that showed they'd been chosen to be read and handled with pleasure. Jacqueline Crozet was an attractive woman in her mid-thirties, with soft eyes and a warm voice. Small and slim, she bore a certain resemblance to Gilles's mother, but without Mona's chic and drive. I found it impossible not to like her.

"You don't sound sure you and Gilles will get married," I said. "There's nothing to stop it now."

"That is precisely what may make it impossible. The horrible way we've been freed to be with each other. That may prove . . ." She frowned and looked down at her hands. "In any case, I don't think Gilles will be ready to see me again for a long time. I hope not forever. First of all, there's his son. He's trying to nerve himself to tell him that his mother is dead."

"I don't envy him that."

"Nor I. It will be especially hard for Gilles. He's not good at handling personal relationships. I think I've helped him there, a little. But perhaps not enough." Jacqueline Crozet raised her head and looked at me again. "And then he has to make his peace with himself. Right now he doesn't like himself. Oh, I know you think he took it coolly. He told me."

"I know he doesn't show his real feelings much."

"It hit him hard, seeing the way you looked at him. Judging him."

"I don't judge my friends," I said. But I felt suddenly uncomfortable, not sure that was the truth.

She continued to look at me probingly. "He didn't like the way he saw himself through your eyes. He'll need time to get over that. He's a sensitive man."

"Too damn sensitive," I growled. "He's got to learn to tolerate friends getting fed up with him sometimes."

"I agree. I hope he learns it soon." She smiled again suddenly. "He'll be hell to live with if I can't lose my temper with him once in a while."

I stood up and said, "It's getting late. I'll go now. Thanks for seeing me."

She rose to her feet. "You haven't questioned me."

"I didn't come for that."

"Why, then?"

"As you said, Gilles and I have known each other a long time. Since we were kids. I'm in Paris, I had a little free time tonight. I wanted to meet you."

"You don't suspect Gilles anymore, then."

"I don't think I ever really did." I held out my hand. She took it and stepped closer and kissed my cheek.

"I hope we do see each other again."

I went out feeling better about Gilles than I had been. I just hoped he'd have the sense to take what fate—good and bad—was offering him.

It was almost midnight when I put my car back in the garage and walked to Place Contrescarpe. There weren't many of the evening's visitors to the neighborhood left around. Most of them were inside the two cafés that were still open on the *place*. There was nobody else walking the poorly lit street leading down to my apartment.

I was only two doors from the fenced courtyard when my nerves warned me, before my eyes did, that something was wrong there.

⊠ 27 ⊠

THERE WAS A *clochard* sleeping on the darkly shadowed sidewalk near the door to my courtyard.

I slid my hand under my jacket and closed it around the grip of the Mauser as I came to a stop.

Clochards do sleep on the sidewalks. On very cold nights, over grills that let heat out of the Métro line below. But there was no grill there, and it was a warm night. In summer the *clochards* of the neighborhood sleep together in the middle of Place Contrescarpe.

This one was curled up in fetal position against the courtyard fence, wrapped in what looked like a raincoat.

I brought the Mauser out.

There was a soft, short whistle from somebody inside a car parked near the *clochard*.

The *clochard* uncurled and came up on one knee with something in his hand.

I almost shot him. But suddenly there was somebody closer to shoot.

Just ahead of me a man stepped out of a dark doorway that I would have passed if I hadn't seen the *clochard*. He twisted toward me with a long-barreled revolver. I put two bullets in him at a distance of four feet, and he settled into an ungainly heap on the sidewalk.

The one who had whistled was leaning out the window of the parked car and turning an automatic rifle in my direction. The *clochard* fired three shots so fast that the explosions blended together. All three .45 slugs hit the man in the face. What was left of his head was kicked back inside the car, taking the rest of him with it.

I was sprinting past the *clochard* to the courtyard door by then, thinking of Fritz alone up there in his apartment. Jean-Marie Reju hissed something at me as I went by him, but I was already punching the buzzer button. The door unlocked and the lamps in the courtyard went on.

The instant the lights went on two shots boomed inside the confines of the courtyard.

I kicked open the door and dodged in, crouched and ready to fire. But there was nobody left to shoot at.

A man sprawled face down across the cobbles with the top of his skull caved in and a little MAC-10 submachine gun lying between his outflung hands. He'd been standing near the tree in the center of the courtyard, facing the door, waiting for me to come through it when the lamps went on.

Fritz was resting his elbows on his living room windowsill with the Beretta still aimed down into the courtyard. He drew the gun back and nodded when I looked up at him.

Reju came in with his open raincoat flapping and lowered his Colt .45 when he saw the dead machine gunner. "Give me your gun and I'll get rid of it," he told me in a no-nonsense whisper. "Get in your apartment fast and go to sleep. It was only me and Donhoff."

Understandably, it was some time before I got to sleep after that. I took off my clothes and put on a bathrobe and bedroom slippers. Then I sat in my living room with the lights out and the windows opened. Over the next couple hours there was a progression of police officers of ever-higher rank converging on the courtyard. I listened to Reju telling them what had happened.

An anonymous phone caller had threatened Fritz Donhoff's life. Fritz had hired Jean-Marie Reju to protect him, and Reju had applied for and obtained a permit to carry a gun while so employed.

Reju had been taking a stroll outside when three men started shooting at him. He had killed the one in the car. The second attacker had been killed when he accidentally stepped into the line of fire and got hit by two bullets that the third man fired at Reju.

The third man had then run away.

Fritz, alarmed by the gunshots, had snatched up his pistol and leaned out his window to see what was happening. The machine gunner in the courtyard had taken aim at him, but luckily Fritz had managed to shoot first. As he had every right to do, defending himself in his own domicile.

And that was all that Reju or Fritz could tell the police about it.

The cops knew more. They had no trouble identifying the two of the dead attackers who still had faces. Both were known *voyous*—hoods who'd done time for robbery, assault, and carrying weapons. They'd also been suspected of killing, but there'd never been witnesses or evidence to convict them.

I heard their names clearly, repeated a number of times by different cops.

At one point I went to my kitchen and poured myself a glass of wine. I sat and sipped it and listened some more. Cops clumped up and down the stairs between Fritz's apartment and the courtyard. Other cops began ringing doorbells and asking people who lived around the courtyard and the street outside if they'd witnessed any of it.

When they came to my apartment I told them the same

things everybody else seemed to be telling them: I'd been awakened by the gunfire, but it had been some time before I'd ventured to look out my windows, and by then it had all been over. I hadn't seen or heard anything that could be of help in their inquiry.

Then I went back to my wine. The house and courtyard seemed unlikely to be free of policemen for the rest of that night. So when I finished the wine I did go to bed.

⊠ **28** ⊠

IT WAS SHORTLY past noon the next day when I got to the headquarters of *La Piscine*—the Swimming Pool.

That's what they used to call the SDECE when it still existed as France's most important foreign intelligence service. The DGSE has taken its place, but it bears the same nickname, and for the same reason. The service has new initials and a different chief. But it handles the same work and operates out of the same facilities in the same location: across the street from a large indoor public swimming pool, the *Piscine des Tourelles*.

I had been out to Orly Airport that morning only to discover that there were no flights between Paris and the Riviera until three P.M. Employees of the Côte d 'Azur Airport had pulled a surprise half-day strike to publicize their demands for higher pay. I phoned the courier service that was supposed to bring the package from Gilles; it would arrive on a four P.M. flight. So I had a leisurely second coffee at Orly, returned to Paris, and went to see Captain Thierry Gallion.

The noon heat was sweltering when I reached the Boulevard Mortier. It's an extra-wide street lined with big maple trees, just inside the eastern limits of Paris. Two military forts loom across the boulevard from each other: the Caserne des Tourelles on one side, the Caserne Mortier on the other. They bear signs warning that this is a military zone where it is forbidden to take photographs.

There's little visible to tempt a photographer. High stone walls topped by crisscrossed steel spikes. Tan-uniformed troopers in black berets and shoes, standing guard with compact automatic rifles before blank steel gates. The top of a radio antenna poking above one fort like a miniature Eiffel Tower.

The headquarters of the DGSE are in the fort on the left, with supplementary facilities in the other across the street.

I drove up Boulevard Mortier between the two forts—and then between the back of the Piscine des Tourelles and the front of the Defense Ministry offices. At the next left turn I went around the tiny Square de Dr. Variot and found a tight parking spot on Avenue Gambetta.

Before climbing out of the Renault I buttoned and adjusted my jacket to make sure the pistol holstered on my shoulder harness didn't show. It was my own Beretta—heavier and bulkier then the Mauser, but Reju had made the smaller gun disappear forever.

I walked back half a block to the little square and entered a café across from the Métro station of the Porte des Lilas. The café was called the Clairon—the Bugler. With a name like that it was a favorite hangout for military types in civilian clothes from the ministry and DGSE. No uniforms, however. The French consider the wearing of military uniforms when off duty in public to be in very poor taste.

I took one of the mica-topped tables near the entrance of the Clarion, between its curve of front windows and the curved bar. For lunch I ordered *choucroute garnie* and a half bottle of Saint-Amour Beaujolais. Then I took a short walk inside the Clarion down a corridor behind one end of the bar.

The corridor led toward a locked rear emergency exit. Halfway along it there was an open doorway on my right and a small table against the wall on my left. Seated at the table, facing toward the front of the café, was a handsome, inoffensive-looking boy of about twenty or twenty-one. He had longish, bright-yellow hair, clear blue eyes, and an athletic build. He wore neatly pressed jeans and a white sport shirt opened at his muscular neck. On the table before him were a pack of cigarettes, a large brown ashtray, a glass of beer, and a black jacket of thin, supple leather that was folded there with apparent carelessness so you wouldn't notice that there was something under it.

He was smoking, and the ashtray was half-filled with the butts of cigarettes he'd consumed. But the beer glass was full, without a trace of head or bubbles; it had been sitting in front of him a long time, untouched. The jacket rested on the left side of his table. That made him a lefty.

I walked past him. Three steps further, close to the emergency exit, there was another open doorway on my right. You couldn't see it until you got there. It opened into an alcove that held a round table with a semicircle of padded banquette. The five men taking their lunch in the alcove were having a quiet, serious discussion until I appeared. They shut up and stared at me without expression.

They ranged in age from late thirties to early fifties. Otherwise they were much alike. Tough, intelligent faces accustomed to exercising authority and assuming the weight of the world. Strong bodies that had known violent exercise but were going soft from too many years behind desks. They were even dressed alike: plain sport shirts and expensive thin leather jackets.

One of them, thirty-nine years old, was going bald and had a hearing aid in his left ear.

"Excuse me," I said, "I'm looking for the toilet."

The one on Thierry Gallion's left pointed and told me, "You passed it. Clearly marked. Next doorway back along the corridor."

"Thank you," I said, and I turned away.

The blond boy was standing now, facing me, blank-faced. The leather jacket that had been carelessly piled on his table was now carelessly draped over his left forearm, concealing his hand and whatever it held. I smiled and walked up to him and turned into the doorway to the toilet.

I stayed in there for about a minute, looking at myself in a mirror hanging askew over the sink. Then I went out. The blond boy was seated at his table again, lighting a new cigarette. His jacket was back on the table, and his beer remained untasted.

My lunch was waiting for me when I got back to the table. The wine was superb. The food wasn't the best, but it wasn't bad. I took my time with it and compensated with the wine.

The blond boy strolled out of the corridor wearing his jacket. His left hand was inside the deep pocket, his other hand dangling, fingers curled. He gave me a bland glance, went outside, and stood there looking up and down the street. I didn't get the impression he missed much. He was pretty enough to make newlywed brides desert their husbands. But I would have been willing to match him against Jean-Marie Reju, even odds. They were different in every way except quiet competence at their shared craft.

The five men from the alcove came out of the corridor. The one with the hearing aid went to the bar and ordered a Perrier. His fellow DGSE executives left the café and turned down Boulevard Mortier toward the forts. The blond boy strolled after them, staying a respectful three paces behind so they could talk without his hearing what they said.

I went to the bar beside Thierry and asked for my bill.

Thierry said, "I have an appointment near the Luxembourg. Half an hour?"

It was a good place for a private talk.

"By the pond," I said. Then I paid my bill, tipped, and went out to my car.

⊠ 29 ⊠

KIDS WERE USING long poles to guide toy boats across the pond behind Luxembourg Palace. Adults who'd brought them there sat on rented chairs, tilting their faces to the sun with closed eyes. Thierry and I walked away from the pond, strolling through the Luxembourg Gardens toward the open marionette theater under the trees.

We walked slowly. His tricky heart forced him to be careful about any form of physical activity. The last time he and his family had crowded my house for a long weekend holiday, back in May, we'd gone swimming. He was all right in the sea as long as he took it easy and got frequent rests floating on his back. The return climb to the house had been hard for him, though. It was a short slope, but steep. He'd had to stop twice before we reached the patio. Then he'd sat there gazing at the horizon and saying nothing. I could see the fast beating of his heart inside his bare chest. Finally he'd gone inside and taken a short nap, and after that he'd been okay.

"Neither of those two names belongs to us," Thierry told me. "So whatever they're up to is no longer any concern of ours."

"No longer," I repeated. I was walking on his left side, to be near his hearing aid. "That means they *were* yours, sometime in the past."

Thierry was silent for a bit, considering what he could tell me without seriously violating official secrecy. "You'll have to tell me why you're interested before I'll say anything further.''

I told him about the setup in the renovated Hotel Dhalsten. ''An illegal surveillance arrangement of that scope, requiring the cooperation of the hotel chain and the construction company that did the renovation, has to be an operation of one of the secret services.''

''It's not ours,'' Thierry said.

We both felt easier after that. If you want potentially damaging information about any government department, the best place to get help is from a rival department.

''Do you know *which* service has it?''

''No,'' Thierry said. But he hesitated. I let that rest for awhile.

''Tell me what you can about Jacques Morel.''

''He served for many years as a member of the former S.A. In Sector Two.''

The S.A. had been the SDECE's *Service Action*. It had stopped existing the same way the SDECE had. Under the DGSE it was called *Division Action*: D.A. The S.A.'s purpose, like that of the D.A., had been to handle dirty work for the service.

Sector Two did the jobs that required stealthy violence. Jobs that have been known to include kidnapping, bombing, and killing.

''His name wasn't Morel in those days,'' Thierry said. Before I could ask, he added, ''I'm not going to tell you his former name. He got in trouble under that name. And he *was* one of ours then.''

We had reached the marionette theater. A large audience of children was shrieking with joy: Punch was beating up a black-jowelled policeman. Thierry and I turned away along a path leading in the direction of the ornate palace

Marie de Medici had built for herself early in the seventeenth century.

"He was highly regarded in the service," Thierry continued. "Entirely a self-made man. Came from a poor background somewhere in the south. With little education and no connections. Joined the army at seventeen and worked his way up to sergeant during the fighting in Algeria. It was there he was recruited into the SDECE."

The struggle between French forces and Algerian rebels had become a particularly vicious one—carried out more in the shadows than in open battle. There was only one job the secret service was likely to have recruited a new man for in that war.

"As a *déménageur*?" Literally the word means a removal man, usually a furniture remover. The underworld has long used it to denote a killer used to remove difficult adversaries. The French secret services have adopted it as a useful euphemism.

Thierry avoided the question. "That was long before my time, of course."

"But you've had a look at his dossier." When he still didn't respond to the question I tried another: "Why was his name changed?"

Thierry considered for a moment. "A man supplying arms and explosives to Corsican insurgents was killed. In another country. I'm not going to give you any more details than that. It caused a *gros pépin*."

Pépin is the pit of an orange or other fruit. It's also slang for "trouble."

"This other country put pressure on France, demanding extradition of the killer. There were repercussions in high places. It was decided that it was best to relieve the pressure by action at a lower level. Against the one who carried out the removal, rather than someone more important who ordered it done. The man you call Jacques Morel was dismissed from the service. Preparations were made to arrest him and turn him over to the other country.''

"Enough to make a man bitter," I said. "And cynical."

"We didn't abandon him," Thierry said defensively. "We enabled him to escape arrest and disappear. The change of name was arranged for him, with everything that might connect him to his former identity erased. In that way, though no longer one of us, he didn't have to worry about the police finding him.''

I said, "And you saw to it the French police didn't really *try* to find him."

"Naturally. But his disappearance had to appear genuine to . . . the other country." There was a slight hesitation. Then he added cautiously, "There was a rumor that shortly thereafter Morel was taken up by the DST. In what capacity, I don't know. It may not be true, of course.''

We both understood. He was giving me the answer to one of my first questions. If Morel worked for the DST, the Hotel Dhalsten operation was DST.

It wouldn't be the first time one of the French services had set up such an operation—and on the Riviera. One had surfaced at the Hotel Majestic in Cannes, when it was revealed that the rooms used by George Ball, U.S. Under Secretary of State, were bugged. It had developed into a *pépin* so *gros* that even French President Giscard d'Estaing had been damaged by it. That operation had been under SDECE control. Its discovery had contributed to the service's fall from grace.

Thierry was probably delighted with the thought that it would be a rival service that would take the heat this time, if the Dhalsten setup surfaced.

I told him, "I need to know Jacques Morel's real name."

He shook his head. "I *told* you . . ."

"I *need* to know," I repeated. And I told him the real reason. I hadn't wanted to. There was the danger Thierry would get so delighted about the opportunity to needle his agency's chief power rival that he wouldn't be able to resist spreading the word. If the DST found out one of its men was playing around with its operation—in a way that could threaten its future existence—Morel was dead. I still needed him alive.

But there was no alternative now. I had to take the risk. Gamble that I'd be able to move faster than Thierry's rumor-spreading. I told him about Crow being in prison for the double murder I was certain Jacques Morel had committed. In the past I'd told Thierry how Crow had saved my life in combat. That was the sort of obligation that meant something to him. He'd been sailing a desk for a long time, but he was still deeply military-minded. For a military man, the friendships and obligations that develop in combat are sacred, overriding almost anything else.

Reluctantly, he said, "I suppose it doesn't matter now. The emergency that made the name change necessary subsided completely a couple years after it arose. No one cares about the incident anymore." Thierry sighed, and frowned, and finally told me, "His name was Jacques Taurenge."

Now I knew. I didn't know if knowing would help, but it was possible. It didn't change my thinking of him as Morel. That was who he was now.

Thierry sat down on a stone bench under a statue of a former queen whose face had weathered beyond recognition. I sat beside him and waited while he drew several slow breaths.

"About the other name you were interested in," he said. "Paul Orain. Known in his own unpleasant circles as Butterfly. I know very little about him. Except that he was, over a short period, one of our honorable correspondents."

The term is the one given by the secret services of France to occasional employees hired from outside their regular staffs. Honorable correspondents are part-time free-lance volunteers, used when needed but with no official connections to government. They include former military officers and respectable civilians whose specialized skills, knowledge, or contacts make them valuable for certain specific assignments. Honorable correspondents also include patriotic gangsters and petty criminals: mercenaries for especially secretive and dirty "commando" missions involving strong-arm work, burglary, sabotage, or removals.

"We dropped him rather quickly," Thierry told me, "when it was learned that he talked too freely when he drank."

"Maybe some other service engaged him."

"I doubt it very much. His reputation as a loudmouth became too well known."

"Did he know Jacques Morel?" I asked.

"It's possible."

I told him the names of the two men the police had recognized among the three who'd been waiting to kill me last night. Thierry gave them some frowning thought, then shook his head.

"I don't recall either of those names. There've been so many over the years."

"I'd appreciate your having a look in your files to see if they're there." I was pretty sure they would be, in the same section of dossiers where he'd turned up the Butterfly. "When do you leave the office this evening?"

"Around seven." Thierry glanced at his watch and stood up. "I have to go now, Pierre-Ange."

"I'll be at my apartment at seven," I told him. "Call me from a public phone somewhere and tell me if you found those two names. I'll stay by my phone till I hear from you."

He nodded. "But please, don't ask me any more favors for a long time after this. Discussions like this aren't good for my nerves."

We shook hands, and he walked off slowly, around the Luxembourg Palace toward Rue de Vaugirard. I went back through the gardens to Rue Soufflot, where I had left my Renault in the parking area alongside the Panthéon.

I was sure it was *more* than possible that the Butterfly had known Morel as an officer of the SDECE. Morel had used him, along with other thugs, in his official capacity with the *Service Action*. He'd have no difficulty in making them believe that anything he asked them to do now, for his own private purposes, was a request from the secret service—and that they were still acting as honorable correspondents.

⊠ **30** ⊠

AT 4 P.M. I was out at Orly waiting for the flight from the Côte d'Azur. It came in twenty minutes late. The courier came off with the package from Gilles and gave it to me. I drove back into Paris, opened the package in Fritz's apartment, and spread its contents on the living room table.

Reju went out for one of his patrols around the neighborhood. Fritz and I divided up Anne-Marie's financial records, going back over the past year. I took on the photostats of her checks. Fritz screwed his monocle into his eye and went to work on her Visa Card statements.

I spent considerable time studying the checks and learned nothing I hadn't already known. She had made a lot of them out to cash. Very little of what had come into her checking account over the period of that year had stayed there longer than a few weeks. I was starting to go over each check again, searching for something whose significance I might have missed the first time, when Fritz spoke.

"There is an odd pattern here."

He lined up the Visa statements, month by month, in sequence. On each month's statement he had underlined a single item with his fountain pen.

"You see?" he said. "The same thing, every month."

Each item he'd underlined was a meal Anne-Marie had charged in a restaurant. The amounts differed slightly. But it was always the same restaurant—in Moustiers-Sainte-Marie, a popular village near the Grand Canyon du Verdon, the most spectacular natural wonder of southern France.

Another thing was the same. I said it: "It's always the last Saturday of the month."

Fritz nodded. "We don't have the statement for July here. But judging by her pattern, she probably ate there again this past Saturday."

"The day before she was murdered."

Fritz looked again at the items he'd marked. "A scheduled appointment . . . for the same time each month. In the restaurant, perhaps. Or elsewhere in or around Moustiers, and she had the meal at the restaurant before or after it."

"Moustiers is a tough two-hour drive from Nice," I mused. "Minimum. A lot of it on those mountain roads around the Verdon gorges. Say two to three hours, depending on weather and road conditions. And the same trip back down. Who did she have to see up there, that she'd use up that much of a day to do it?"

"That," Fritz agreed, "is the question."

We were both thinking the same answer. But I shook my head.

"Anne-Marie and Jacques Morel both lived in Nice. Why would he arrange to meet her that far away?"

"There is always a reason," Fritz said. "This one we simply don't know as yet."

I used his phone to call Gilles in Nice and told him, "Anne-Marie went up to Moustiers the last Saturday of every month over the last year. Do you know about that?"

"No, I don't."

"She'd be gone for most of the day, Gilles. You must have noticed."

"Anne-Marie often went off without me," he said, tight-voiced. "Sometimes she would explain she'd made new

friends. She seldom told me about them, and after a time
I ceased being interested. I long ago stopped paying attention to where she went, or when, or for how long.''

At seven that evening I was in my own apartment waiting impatiently for that call from Thierry Gallion.

It didn't come until half past.

''Those last two names you gave me,'' he said, being
careful even over a pay phone. ''They were very much like
that other one we discussed. Used for a period and then
dropped. Because they couldn't be depended on to be discreet.''

''Thierry,'' I said, ''you told me our friend Jacques came
from someplace in the south. Do you remember *where* in
the south?''

''A village called Châteauneuf,'' he answered promptly.
''I remember being amused when I came across that in his
dossier. There are so very *many* places of that name in
France.''

''Where is this one?'' I asked him.

''That I didn't notice. Or at any rate I don't recall the
exact location. Just somewhere in the south.''

I put down the phone. Châteauneuf—''Newcastle,'' in
English. Thierry had touched on the problem: there must
have been a hundred of them sprinkled all over France. All
were named that when they were newly built, but they were
now invariably very old. I took an atlas of southeastern France
from one of my bookcases and got a detailed map of the
Alpes Maritimes and a magnifying glass from my desk.

Jean-Marie Reju was in the kitchen heating another dinner left by one of the local ladies when I reentered Fritz
Donhoff's living room. I told Fritz the name and gave him
the atlas. Spreading the map on his table, I focused the
magnifier on Moustiers and then began slowly circling it

and the Verdon gorges. I found it: one of the villages noted in the smallest print.

"Here's one," I told Fritz. "About a thirty- or forty-minute drive from Moustiers. It's called Châteauneuf-de-Soleils."

Fritz found it in the atlas: "Population 365. One church, one castle ruin, one small hotel. The hotel is a surprise, in a village so tiny."

It was an area of France he didn't know. Though born in Munich, he'd spent most of his life in Paris and seldom ventured far from it. A city man. I told him, "People come from all over France to look at the gorges of the Verdon Canyon. Not many foreigners. But enough French to fill every hotel, trailer park, and camping site in the area. They build hotels in some unlikely places, and never enough. Taking care of all the sightseers is the main industry there."

"Sounds overcrowded."

"It's a big area. Plenty of wild, empty space left. You get into those gorges, or into the hills away from the main road, and you won't see a house for miles. Moustiers is the only crowded town. It has the most hotels and restaurants. A good place for Morel to watch Anne-Marie without being seen until he made sure nobody else was watching."

"We are assuming," Fritz said, "that *this* Châteauneuf, near to Moustiers, is the one Jacques Morel originally came from. When his name was Jacques Taurenge."

"It fits the situation."

"It does," Fritz acknowledged. "All right, then—he comes from there. And he has a place there. One he goes to stay at from time to time. On weekends, usually."

"So he picks Moustiers for Anne-Marie to come to with her blackmail payments—because it's close to his place, but not too close."

''And we now understand *how* she contacted Morel after Lotis phoned her about Pilon. The last Saturday of the month was her day to meet him.''

''The timing was right: Lotis called her Wednesday to warn her of Pilon. She didn't have any way to get in touch with Morel until Saturday. That's when she went up there to meet him. It was probably the first time she told him what she'd done to get some of the money for him. It scared him—and the next night she and Pilon died to cover his tracks.''

Fritz said, ''They probably met at lunchtime. Noon to two P.M. Between then and the following night would be enough time for Morel to make his plans and assemble his helpers: local ones and some from Paris. He almost certainly told them it was a job for the secret service.''

''Morel must have returned to Nice with Anne-Marie,'' I said. ''To supervise what followed. He had her phone Crow to make that lunch date with him on Sunday—and to use Crow's house that night. Morel didn't have anything against Crow. He just wanted a way to point the murder investigation in the wrong direction.''

Fritz nodded. ''And once your friend Crow agreed to let her use his house, she phoned Pilon and told him to meet her there. Saying she had information to give him. Morel didn't have to explain much to her about why he wanted her to do this. Beyond telling her it was part of a plan to get the threat of Pilon off both of them.''

''Maybe not even that,'' I said. ''Morel had her under his thumb. He might even have been holding a gun on her by the time she made the call to Pilon.''

''That's quite possible, if he had her in Crowley's house by then. He, and probably some of his helpers.''

''Before Pilon got to the house, Morel held a gun on her

and forced her to strip and pose for those Polaroid pictures.''

''Or it may be,'' Fritz suggested, ''that he took those pictures of her long ago. Money may not have been the only sort of blackmail payment Morel demanded of her. He sounds to me like one of those who enjoys toying with people.''

The cold hatred I felt for Morel was getting stronger with every word.

Back and forth, Fritz and I worked out the probable sequence from that point on.

I was certain Anne-Marie knew that Crow kept a gun in the house. Everyone in the family knew it. Morel found it and killed her with it. Then he and his ''honorable correspondents'' waited for Pilon. Whatever explanation Morel gave his helpers for what they were doing, it wouldn't have to be elaborate. Secret service officers don't tell their mercenaries much about the reason for a dirty job. It's sufficient that the service has deemed it necessary for the security of the nation.

Pilon came to the house—and into their trap. He had no reason to be more wary than usual. All he knew of what he was investigating at that point was that it involved a violation of business ethics. Nothing big enough to kill for, ordinarily. Certainly nothing that would pull in professional removers.

They'd forced him to strip at gunpoint, and then they'd killed him. Again, with Crow's gun. Which was then hidden where it was sure to be found eventually.

Then Morel and his men left the house and headed for Nice. On the way one of them phoned the La Turbie gendarmerie and reported hearing gunshots from the house. In Nice they divided up the jobs of planting the photos of Anne-Marie in Crow's studio and removing evidence of what Pilon had been working on from his office and apartment. With helpers like Butterfly, at least one of them had to be as skilled as Morel at dealing with locks.

"All of it feels right to me," Fritz Donhoff said finally. "Now—how are you going to prove all or any of it?"

"I don't think I can," I told him. "I'm going to have to do something else."

⊠ **31** ⊠

I COULDN'T GET space on a plane for that night. A common problem with flights to the Riviera in the summer. The first seat available was at half past ten in the morning. I booked it.

At noon the next day I was leaving the Côte de'Azur Airport wearing sunglasses to counter the ferocity of the sunlight. I hadn't left my car there this time. The bomb at my house had discouraged me from taking even small risks that could be avoided. The Peugeot was in a Nice garage I'd never used before.

I had the cab that took me into Nice stick to heavy traffic that discouraged attack. I jumped out at Rue Massena, a pedestrian shopping street where any car tailing the cab couldn't come in after me. Walking through it swiftly, I cut over to the taxi stand at Place Grimaldi. There were two cabs there. I paid the first to take a short cruise empty and used the second to lose anyone who'd followed me through Rue Massena on foot.

At half past noon I was back in my Peugeot, and the gun holstered under my arm was once more Heckler & Koch's P7.

Ten minutes later I was onto the A8 autoroute heading west. I left the autoroute above Saint Tropez and drove up route N555 toward the Grand Canyon du Verdon. The smell of the sea faded and the aroma of mountain pine forests took over. The sun stayed strong, but the air got cooler.

The Verdon Grand Canyon has no resemblence to Arizona's. It's long and twisty and narrow—so narrow in places you can throw a stone across. It took me almost two hours to get there—and then almost another hour, taking the Corniche Sublime with its views of the river battering sheer cliffs a thousand feet below, to reach Moustiers.

I left the Peugeot in the parking area behind the church of Sainte Anne and walked over the short bridge crossing the ravine that divides the village in half. The restaurant where Anne-Marie had charged all those meals was on the main *place*.

The normal lunch hour was past. The owner was helping a waiter prepare tables for later diners. I showed them Anne-Marie's picture. They recognized her immediately. Restaurants in Moustiers don't get many repeat customers. For most of the French, a voyage to the Grand Canyon du Verdon is a once-in-a-lifetime affair.

She always took lunch at a table by the big window looking out on the *place*, they told me. They even remembered her first name was Anne-Marie because at some time during her lunch a man would phone and ask for that name. She would go to the phone and take the call, listening and saying little. After the call she would return to her table. Sometimes to finish her lunch. But more often she left the meal unfinished and had a large brandy instead. Then she would go out—they didn't know where.

The routine wasn't hard to figure. It gave Morel an opportunity to watch her enter the village and then to observe her in the restaurant. He'd mingle with sightseers in the *place* until certain nobody else had her under surveillance. Then he would phone and tell her where to go. A different collection point each time. Along one of the back roads that got little traffic. He'd get there first and take up a position where he could observe Anne-Marie's approach.

When he was sure she was alone he'd step out and stop her. She'd pay him off and drive away, back down to Nice.

I asked for directions to Châteauneuf. The owner got out a local map and showed me. The château from which the village derived its name was marked as a ruin, on a slope near a waterfall. It and the original village around it, I was told, had been partially destroyed by a landslide in the previous century and abandoned. A newer village had been built a few hundred yards away, lower on the slope.

I went back to my car and drove there.

It was a cheerless little village on the bank of a narrow mountain stream at the bottom of a gorge that got little sun. The houses huddled together for protection against the sharp, cold winds that cut through the gorge. Their walls were of dark stone, their steep roofs covered with black slate. The one-lane road that led to the village continued past it for about two hundred yards. It ended at the foot of a waterfall that was the only lovely aspect of the gorge—high and slim, with the water cascading over humps of rock like moving lace.

The small hotel didn't look bad. It was the newest building in the village, roofed with orange tiles, its walls white-washed with red trim around the windows. I checked in, taking a room for one night. It was the quickest and most natural way to become accepted as a temporary part of the village.

The reception desk was inside the hotel's barroom, the only one in the village. The hotel's manager, a young, stocky red-haired woman with a broad face and lively eyes, also tended the bar. She was pouring a glass of red wine for a farmer when I came in. After I'd signed in and paid she went back to gossip with him while I carried my bag through a door behind the bar and up a short flight of stairs.

The room was like the rest of the hotel: small and sparsely furnished, but clean. I left my bag on the bed and went back down to the bar.

The redhead and the farmer stopped their chat to look at me, she with a friendly smile, he neither friendly nor un-friendly, just curious. He was a tough-looking old man with gnarled hands and a seamed face, wearing a cloth cap, overalls, a turtleneck shirt, and rubber boots caked with mud.

His glass of red was almost empty. I sat on the stool next to him and asked if I could buy him another. He finished his wine and said, with dignity, "That would be kind."

I ordered the same and began spinning a tale about com-ing up there to get away from family tensions for a while. My tale included a wife who complained that my job as a bus driver didn't bring in enough money and a couple of kids who were always watching television and who paid no attention to whatever I told them. The farmer and the redhead listened with interest, nodding sympathetically. The quickest way to relax the French is to tell them so many intimate details about yourself that they can't regard you as a stranger.

"There's a man I know down in Nice," I said when I had them warmed up, "who comes from here. Name's Jacques Taurenge."

"Oh, sure," the red-haired hotel manager said. "He comes to his place most weekends. Only he calls himself Morel now. It *used* to be Taurenge—but he says he never liked the name, so he changed it."

"Don't blame him," the farmer said. "Wasn't nothing about that family to be proud of. Mother that ran off with some man passing through and never came back. Father drunk all the time, right up to the day he died."

"That was before my time," the redhead said. "He left before I was born. Only came back about four years ago."

The farmer said, "I never liked Jacques when he was a kid, and I still don't like him much. But it was a shame. Kid was always dressed in rags. Going down around Moustiers to scrounge stuff out of the trash. To steal a little, too, I guess. Father never gave him anything except beatings."

The redhead said, "Well, he's sure done well for himself since then." She looked at me inquiringly. "Must be worth a fortune now, whatever it is he does for a living. Is he married, do you know?" The question embarrassed her. "I mean, he never talks about that, either."

"I don't know," I told her. "I've just met him a few times. Bar in Nice. He does all right for himself, I think."

The redhead nodded reflectively. "He must. All it's costing him to fix up the old château."

"One thing I got to hand him," the farmer said grudgingly. "I remember when he was a kid, the way he'd go up there to hang around the old château. Then come down and boast about how he'd come back someday with enough to buy it for himself. Fix it up to look like a real castle again. And there he is, back and doing it. Got to give him that—even if he's a fool, spending that much on it and no end to it."

The redhead's mind still seemed preoccupied with Morel's possible marriage potential. "It must have cost him a fortune just to run those electric and phone lines up there."

I said, "He told me I ought to have a look at his place, if I ever got up here. How do I find it?"

They told me: to the end of the road by the waterfall, and then up an unpaved route to the ruins of the old village.

A fairly new pickup truck pulled to a stop outside the hotel. The redhead glanced at it and then made a quick warning sign to the farmer, finger to her lips. The farmer gave a low laugh.

A plump man in his late thirties got out of the pickup and came into the bar. He wore dungarees and a good leather jacket. His expensive cowboy boots made him look taller than he was. He also wore a surly expression that looked habitual. Pointedly ignoring the farmer and me, he settled on a stool at the end of the bar, as far from us as he could get, and ordered Armagnac.

The farmer winked at me and turned to him. "Antoine, we were just talking about Jacques. About what a fool he is, spending all that money to fix up that wreck. This here's a friend of his from Nice."

Antoine turned his head and looked at me for the first time. "You're a friend of Jacques?"

"Not really," I said. "I've only met him a few times."

He eyed me suspiciously. "What's your name?"

I told him. Having registered under my own, I couldn't give him another. And I wasn't sure I wanted to.

"Never heard of you."

The farmer told him, "Jacques wouldn't introduce his friends to *you*. Anyway, he never brings them up here, and you never go anywhere else. Too lazy to."

Antoine looked away from us and sipped his drink, pointedly ignoring our presence again.

The farmer couldn't resist needling him further: "Like we were saying, Jacques could've built himself a nice new modern house for less than half what he's spent so far on that château of his. And it's still mostly a ruin." Not a lover of antiquity, apparently. He went on with it: "Of course, all the people around here doing that restoration work for Jacques are glad to have him back. Glad to see his money."

Antoine gulped down the rest of his drink, tossed money

on the bar, and stalked out, his face ruddy with suppressed anger. Outside, he turned to the left and vanished from sight, leaving his pickup truck parked out front.

The farmer laughed softly. "Jacques's kid cousin. Only relative he's got left alive, far as I know. Lazy bum. No good for anything except hunting. Used to work sometimes down in Moustiers, when he had to. Now he doesn't have to. Jacques takes care of him. Pays for his food, clothes, his place here in town. *And* fixed him up a room in the ruins near the château so he can stay up there nights."

"Antoine doesn't get all that for doing nothing," the barmaid reminded him. "He works for Jacques as his caretaker."

The farmer shrugged. "Not much work in a job like that."

I looked at my watch, taking note of the exact time.

The farmer finished his second glass of red. I bought him another, paid for our drinks, and strolled out.

32

MOREL'S COUSIN ANTOINE was not in sight. I went to my car and got a few items out of the back, putting them where they'd be handy.

I was sitting on the front steps of the hotel when Antoine emerged from a narrow passage between two dark stone houses. He saw me but made a show of having no interest in me as he walked quickly back to his pickup truck. He climbed into the cab and drove off, going toward the waterfall at the end of the road.

I let the truck get farther away before getting into the Peugeot and starting it. When Antoine turned up onto the dirt road I went after him.

He was halfway up the dirt road when I came onto it. I gunned after him and caught up as he neared the ruins of the original village. Churning clouds of dust, I passed him and then cut over in front of the truck, blocking it. Antoine jammed on the brakes so hard the truck stalled.

I jumped out of the Peugeot and sprinted back as Antoine twisted around in the seat of the cab, reaching down for something behind it. He was picking up a hunting rifle when I poked the P7 through his open window and stuck it in his ear.

I said, "Let it go."

He let it go.

I opened his door and stepped back. "Get out."

He climbed out, his surly face scared. "What do you want? There's no money or—"

"Turn around and put your hands behind your back. Don't make me wait. If you make me nervous, I'll shoot you."

Antoine turned quickly, hands behind him. From my pocket I took one of the items I'd gotten out of the back of the car. A pair of handcuffs. I locked them on his wrists. Then I said, "Now let's go up to the château."

He led the way, climbing awkwardly with his arms pulled behind him. The rockslide had plowed straight through the middle of the original village, flattening most of its houses. Some giant boulders still rested there, rising higher than the ruins. Several houses on either side had escaped the main force of the slide. But neglect and looting over the century since had turned them into wrecks, too.

One of the smallest houses had a door and windows, as well as a roof. It was the only one that did. That would be for Antoine when he stayed there on guard duty. We went through a space between it and a boulder up to the château.

It had once been a long, majestic structure. The slide had wiped out all of the left wing. But part of the right wing, with its square tower, remained. Restoration work on this section was extensive. New blocks of stone raised the big tower to its original height. It had been roofed with gray slate, and all of its windows were new. The rest of the right wing connecting to the tower was in various stages of repair.

A gravel driveway led to the last part of this wing, where a wide opening had been cut through a wall. Whatever the function of that part of the château had been, it was now being converted into a garage. Antoine led me into it. There was a floor of poured concrete and new rafters, but no roof as yet. It was big enough to take three cars.

We went through the back of the garage onto a patio of crushed stone and crossed to a house attached to the tower. It was roofed, with shuttered windows and recent masonry work around a stout oak door with two locks.

"Where are the keys?" I asked Antoine.

He hesitated, struggling between fear and duty.

One of the items I'd gotten from the back of the car was a crowbar I'd stuck down through my belt. I tugged it out and said, "I can break in. But if you're going to make me work like that, I'll use this on you first."

"In my left pants pocket," Antoine told me.

I dug a ring of keys from his pocket and found the two that worked the locks. We entered a wide hallway. Its cement floor had been laid in but not covered, the walls plastered but not painted. An interior archway led between a totally modern kitchen and bathroom and then into a vast living room and dining area that took up much of the ground floor of the tower.

It had been entirely restored and renovated and comfortably furnished. Oriental carpets on the parquet floors, paneled walls, a rebuilt curve of stairway leading to the floor above. I opened the shutters of a wide set of windows on one side to let in the daylight. The windows framed a beautiful view of the waterfall.

I turned around and looked at the piece of furniture that interested me most: a television set.

It had a top-brand videocassette player connected to it. But there were no videocassettes in evidence anywhere in the room.

Until that moment I couldn't be sure I'd come to the right place. All I'd known was that Jacques Morel had to keep his blackmail ammunition hidden somewhere. Preferably far removed from the Hotel Dhalsten.

"Your cousin Jacques has a stock of videocassettes here," I said to Antoine. "Where does he keep them?"

He said, "I don't know."

I brandished the crowbar, and he squealed, "I *don't* know! I swear it! I never saw anything like that!"

I believed him. Morel wouldn't trust Antoine with the secret of his prosperity. "He has to have a private storage place," I said. "Where he keeps things he doesn't want you or anybody else to touch."

Antoine drew a ragged breath, fighting it out in his guts. It was a short fight. He told me, "There's a cellar room under this one. I've never been down there. He keeps it locked all the time. I don't have a key to that—I *swear* I don't."

I looked around the living room. "Where's the door to it?"

He nodded his head toward the stairway. "Under there. The floor."

I lowered the crowbar and went under the stairway. A rug covered the floor there. I flipped it up with my foot. There was a trapdoor with a solid lock.

I told Antoine to sit on the floor in a corner of the living room, facing the walls. He had trouble lowering himself all the way with his wrists fastened behind him. But finally he settled into place.

I used the crowbar to break open the locked trapdoor. Getting a flat flashlight from my jacket, I shone it down through the opening. There was a flight of wooden steps, recently installed and unpainted, leading down to what had probably once been part of a small underground crypt. Two steel filing cabinets stood against a wall down there.

I looked at my watch.

Then I told Antoine, "I'm going to have a look. If I come up and see you've moved, I'll kill you."

He made a sound like a repressed groan. He didn't turn his head to look in my direction.

I went down the steps. The drawers of the cabinets were locked. I broke one open. It was filled with video-cassettes.

Each cassette was neatly labeled, but in a code I couldn't interpret. I broke open the rest of the drawers. One had more cassettes. The rest were empty—ready to receive future cassettes.

I carried five cassettes up to the living room. Antoine hadn't budged from his corner. I turned on the TV and its videocassette player and inserted one of the cassettes.

I played a short part of it, and then a little of each of the other four. All of the recorded scenes had taken place in what looked like rooms in the Hotel Dhalsten. In some sequences the hotel's distinctive monogram showed up on bathroom towels or bed covers.

One involved an often-photographed German industrialist and two striking-looking young hookers, one male, the other female. I didn't recognize the people in the other scenes I played, but in some one could infer what the participants were from what was said. Like the one in which two officials of an African government discussed how to assassinate their country's present dictator. But most of the scenes involved misconduct of either a sexual or business nature.

I had what I'd come for.

Going into the kitchen, I rummaged through drawers and found a roll of large plastic garbage bags. I took one and went back to the living room, dumped in the five cassettes, climbed down through the trapdoor, and filled the bag with the rest of the cassettes. Carrying it up into the living room, I set it on the floor and looked at my watch again.

Just over an hour had passed since Antoine had stalked out of the hotel's bar.

I took out my gun, walked over to Antoine, and told him to turn around. When he did, I aimed the P7 at his face.

"What did your cousin Jacques tell you when you called him after you left the bar?"

He looked up into the dark mouth of the gun, his eyes almost crossing. Weakly, he whispered, "He said for me to get up here with my rifle and keep you away from the house."

"Until he got here," I added.

Antoine nodded unhappily.

I helped him to his feet, holding the gun on him while I used my free hand to unlock the cuffs and slip them back in my pocket. Then I took him over to the trapdoor and sent him down the steps into the room under it.

"Stay quiet down there until I let you out," I warned him. I closed the trapdoor, dragged over a heavy chest of drawers, and dumped it on top. Antoine wasn't going anywhere until I came back.

I picked up the bag of videocassettes and carried it down to my car. Then I drove back to Moustiers.

In addition to being a center for visitors to the Grand Canyon du Verdon, Moustiers is renowned for its glazed pottery. I bought a cardboard packing carton from one of the pottery houses and stuffed the bag of cassettes in it. Tearing a page from my notebook, I wrote instructions on it, put them inside with the cassettes, and sealed the carton with tape. I wrote the name and address of Denise Berri on the outside of the carton and carried it to the bus park on the edge of the town.

Denise Berri was an Air-Inter hostess who lived in Nice and flew the airbus shuttle between there and Paris. We'd gotten friendly over the past four years, and we'd lunched together with Fritz Donhoff in Paris when we'd been there at the same time.

The note inside told her that if I didn't pick up the carton from her before her next morning's flight, I wanted her to deliver it to Fritz. He would know how to make use of the cassettes, if I wasn't around to do it. The note also asked Denise to give the bearer of the carton two hundred francs, which either I or Fritz would repay.

My timing was good. The tour buses that bring sight-seers up from the Riviera to the Grand Canyon of Verdon always stop at Moustiers to give their passengers time to eat and shop. Two of the buses at the park were scheduled to begin their return trip to Nice in half an hour.

I gave one of the drivers two hundred francs and told him about the other two hundred he'd get when he delivered the carton to Denise Berri. He took the carton from me with a pleased smile. I'd made his day.

I drove back to the village of Châteauneuf but stopped before reaching the little hotel and turned off the road into a grove of trees. When the car was in far enough so it couldn't be seen from the road I got out. I walked the rest of the way to the waterfall and up the dirt road, moving fast. The timing was getting close.

When I reached Antoine's pickup truck I took out his hunting rifle and checked to make sure it was fully loaded. I carried it with me up to the château and inside the tower living room.

Dragging the chest away, I opened the trapdoor and let Antoine climb out. Then I used the handcuffs again, this time to shackle his wrists to one of the stairway's balusters.

"You should be able to break that in an hour or so," I told him, "if you put all your weight to work on it. However," I added, "there's likely to be some shooting around here before long. I wouldn't advise you to get loose before that's over."

I walked outside and surveyed the terrain around the château. Then I looked at my watch.

Jacques Morel would be showing up soon. Probably with whatever honorable correspondents he had left.

⊠ **33** ⊠

He came shortly after eight that evening. At that time of year it was still full daylight.

Two other men arrived first. Only two. The attrition rate among Morel's troops had become fierce lately.

The two left their car beside the pickup truck and began their climb up the rest of the slope on foot, spreading apart and crouching as they neared the original village, using its ruins and the rockslide to cover their approach. One had a rifle, the other a repeating shotgun.

They disappeared inside the village ruins, one swinging to his right around the rockslide, the other to the left between the roofless, broken-walled houses.

Then Jacques Morel appeared, climbing a heavily wooded slope behind the ridge above the château. He was carrying his rifle, which had a telescopic sight. When he reached the ridge Morel eased into position between a rock spur and a boulder and stayed there. From there he had a vantage point overlooking all of the slope that held the château and the broken village.

It had been predictable. That was his mode of operation. Send his troops in first to pin down the enemy. Then come in over the high ground, from which he could make sure the job got finished properly.

His two-man team emerged from the broken village. They advanced slowly up the slope toward the château.

Keeping well apart, using bushes, rocks, and trees for cover.

Morel stayed where he was, observing, waiting for his helpers to flush me out or make me reveal my position down there by firing at them.

I stepped out from behind a jut of rock with Antoine's rifle, twenty yards to his left, and said, "Morel . . ."

He *could* have done the sensible thing: frozen in position and dropped his weapon. But he didn't. What he did was hurl himself to one side, dropping toward the ground as he twisted to fire at me with his own rifle.

He was fast. But not that fast.

I shot him in the chest, dead center. Morel was kicked against the base of the boulder, the force of impact jarring the rifle out of his hands.

He slid down on his knees and then surged up again, staring at where his rifle had fallen. It lay a few yards from him. Morel tried to go to it. But his legs didn't have enough left in them for that kind of work. He sagged back against the boulder, bracing himself there to stay up, his hands pressing hard against the place where my bullet had penetrated his chest.

The two men below had come to a halt. Staying low. Squinting up past the château, trying to make out what was happening on the ridge.

I fired four fast shots down the slope at them, driving them back to better cover. They would start to work their way up again, but slowly, having to find cover all the way. Well before they could reach the ridge I would be gone down that other slope Morel had used to come up. Heading back to my car.

I walked to Jacques Morel. He was sliding down the side of the boulder, sagging to his spread knees. His hands, still pressed against his chest, were wet with blood.

I gazed down at him, my face so stiff it hurt, thinking of the year of hell he'd given Anne-Marie before finally ending it with two bullets.

Morel glared up at me with dimming eyes. He tried to say something, but all that came out of his mouth was a froth of pink bubbles.

"What you didn't understand," I told him, "is that I don't need you alive anymore."

I didn't leave until he was dead.

⊠ 34 ⊠

ON THE FOLLOWING Monday, at a few minutes before noon, I was on the Rue de la Gendarmerie, across from the main gate of the Nice prison.

I had plenty of company there. Mostly women, some with children and babies, waiting for afternoon visiting hours so they could go into the prison to see husbands, fathers, sons.

At noon a door in the gate opened. The families began filing in to visit the prisoners. I stood there waiting for a prisoner to come out.

It was twenty minutes past noon when Crow emerged.

Nathalie was at his side, clutching his arm, looking happy but dazed.

Arlette was on his other side, wearing a puzzled frown. They crossed the street to me.

"The *juge d'instruction* even *apologized* to Crow," Nathalie told me. "He said he'd made an honest mistake, and he hoped we'd forgive any inconvenience he's caused us. That is actually what he called it—an *inconvenience*."

Crow was squinting at me thoughtfully. "You look tired."

I said, "I've been working a little too hard."

"In a good cause," he said. And then: "How'd you do it?"

I shrugged. "Had a heart-to-heart with Escorel. Persuaded him of the error of his ways."

"Sure you did." Crow reached out and put a hand against my chest. "See you, buddy." Then he put his arm around Nathalie and walked off with her toward her car.

Arlette and I stayed behind, watching them go.

"All right," Arlette said, "now tell me. How *did* you do it?"

I told her about getting hold of Morel's videocassettes—and about what had happened to Morel.

She stared at me. "You deliberately tricked him into a situation where you had an excuse to kill him. Coldly and calculatingly."

I didn't speak of the cold, calculating things Morel had done to Anne-Marie and to the others he'd been blackmailing. Instead I said, "He didn't have to try shooting me. He could have given up—and waited for the DST to kill him."

Arlette moved her shoulders as though to rid herself of the kind of chill that comes with a bad dream. She said, "Tell me the rest of it."

"I know somebody in the DGSE. I went to Paris, and he put me in touch with his opposite number in the DST."

"And you gave him those cassettes to look at."

"Not all of them," I told her. "I'm holding a few of the most incriminating ones back until I'm absolutely certain Crow will stay free. I explained that to the man I met. I didn't have to explain what would happen if certain friendly foreign governments learn the French government has been collecting damaging material about their diplomats and business tycoons."

"The DST would go the way of the old SDECE," Arlette said. "And the Interior Minister might fall like the Defense Minister did."

"I imagine the man I spoke to discussed it with someone higher up in the DST. Who probably explained the problem to someone high in the Interior Ministry. Who in turn persuaded *juge d'instruction* Escorel to drop his case against Crow. It's that simple.''

"Oh, sure. Simple. Except that nobody can make a *juge d'instruction* do anything he doesn't want to. Because nobody can take a case away from him once he's on it.''

I said, "Except that in Xavier Escorel's case, he has political ambitions. I understand he's smart enough to realize his future won't be so bright if high levels of government come to feel he's an uncooperative type. Like I said, simple.''

Arlette said, "You really are an unscrupulous man." There might have been a certain amount of grudging admiration in there somewhere.

"I have scruples," I said. "About letting a friend do a long prison stretch for something he didn't do.''

Arlette nodded. "I give you that. You did get him free. I have ambivalent feelings about it, though. As an attorney, my job is to save a client. No matter how, as long as it's legal. But there *is* an old value around. Much misused and neglected, I admit. But still important. It's called the truth.''

"In this case," I told her, "the truth wasn't available in any form that would get Crow out.''

I took her arm and led her away from the prison. "It's over a week since you promised to go for that swim with me. I think we can both take the time for it now.''

We went to my place but didn't get around to going down for that swim until after the sun had set. Which made it the night swim we'd originally talked about. We spent a long time in the warm sea. When we came out and started back up the path to the house I looked at the beads of water on her dark skin, each drop reflecting the moon.

"A vision of delight," I told her.

"For a cold, calculating man, you do have something warm in there somewhere, Pierre-Ange. Reserved for special occasions, of course."

"Ah, you've noticed."

Arlette squeezed my hand in hers. "Indeed, indeed . . ."

We found Crow and Nathalie seated at my patio table waiting for us. There was a bottle of champagne and four glasses on the table.

"Thought we'd drop by for a spot of celebration," Crow said, and he went to work on the bottle's foil and wire.

"Mona and Gilles send their love," Nathalie told me. "They've gone up to get Alain—and to break the news to him together. It's not going to be an easy time for them for a while. But they'll come to see you, too, when they can."

Crow popped the cork and poured. We raised our glasses in a silent toast.

There was no sound but the cry of a hawk, circling in search of prey somewhere in the dark above us—and the clink of our four glasses meeting.

About the Author

Marvin H. Albert was born in Philadelphia and has lived in New York, Los Angeles, London, Rome, and Paris. He currently lives on the French Riviera with his wife, the French artist Xenia Klar. He has two children, Jan and David.

He has been a Merchant Marine Officer, actor, theatrical road manager, newspaperman, magazine editor, and Hollywood script writer. In addition, he is the author of numerous books of fiction and non-fiction.

Several of Mr. Albert's novels have been Literary Guild choices, and he has been honored with a Special Award by the Mystery Writers of America. Nine of his books have been made into motion pictures.

BACK IN THE REAL WORLD is the second book in the *Stone Angel* series.